The Curse of Caste; or The Slave Bride

THE CURSE OF CASTE;
OR THE SLAVE BRIDE

A Rediscovered African American Novel

BY JULIA C. COLLINS

Edited by William L. Andrews
and Mitch Kachun

OXFORD
UNIVERSITY PRESS

2006

OXFORD

UNIVERSITY PRESS

Oxford University Press, Inc., publishes works that
further Oxford University's objective of excellence
in research, scholarship, and education.

Oxford New York
Auckland Cape Town Dar es Salaam Hong Kong Karachi
Kuala Lumpur Madrid Melbourne Mexico City Nairobi
New Delhi Shanghai Taipei Toronto

With offices in
Argentina Austria Brazil Chile Czech Republic France Greece
Guatemala Hungary Italy Japan Poland Portugal Singapore
South Korea Switzerland Thailand Turkey Ukraine Vietnam

Published by Oxford University Press, Inc.
198 Madison Avenue, New York, NY 10016
www.oup.com

Oxford is a registered trademark of Oxford University Press

Library of Congress Cataloging-in-Publication Data
Collins, Julia C., d. 1865.
The curse of caste; or The slave bride : a rediscovered African American novel
/ by Julia C. Collins ; edited by William L. Andrews and Mitch Kachun.
p. cm.
Includes bibliographical references.

ISBN-13: 978-0-19-530160-1 (pbk.)

1. Racially mixed people—Fiction. 2. Family secrets—Fiction.
3. New Orleans—Fiction. I. Andrews, William L., 1946– .
II. Kachun, Mitchell A. (Mitchell Alan). III. Title.
IV. Title: Curse of caste. V. Title: Slave bride.
PS1359.C563C65 2006
813'.6—dc22
2006007859

Printed in the United States of America
on acid-free paper

Contents

Foreword

The volume that you hold in your hands contains two stories. One is the suspenseful novel written by Julia C. Collins. It was published in thirty-one installments in *The Christian Recorder* between February 25 and September 23, 1865. The Civil War was ending; Constitutional amendments were abolishing slavery and defining people of African descent as United States citizens with (almost) the same rights as citizens of any other heritage. The story is full of twists and turns of love, identity, and family conflict. In and of itself it is a compelling and delightful read—at least until the end when what we really want to know remains untold.

The volume you hold is exemplary evidence of where we are now and where others will be going in the future. It tells a story of how more such stories might be found, validated, and interpreted. It shows how far we have come in the process of reclaiming and understanding the lives and letters of people who lived before us. The end of this rediscovery story is also untold, but that is not a bad thing at all. Hopefully, your reading of *The Curse of Caste* and the story of literary sleuthing that its introduction and other appended material provide will cause many of you to join in the search.

William L. Andrews and Mitch Kachun do not claim to be the first to have rediscovered *The Curse of Caste*. Rather, their work is a prime example of scholarly collaboration and sharing. They deliberately looked for other people who knew about *The Curse of Caste*, about *The Christian Recorder* in which it appeared, about Julia C. Collins and about others who wrote during her time and published in similar venues. In the process of researching Julia Collins and preparing for this edition, they shared their findings, and, in turn, others shared information with them. They participated on panels at professional conferences with others who were working on Julia Collins and similar rediscovered authors. These sessions were often lively and inspiring. The results go beyond this book. Articles and special issues of professional journals devoted to African American archival research and to writings by and about Julia C. Collins are already in the works. It is hoped that this will lead to discovery of more rich and varied literature, to better scholarship and literary interpretation, and to more readers of what has already proven to be useful for our present-day pleasure and instruction.

We are grateful to these two for bringing us the suspenseful, page-turner story made even more so by the absence of its ending. And, with thanks, we accept their "Alternate Conclusions" with explanations for why Collins may have chosen to end the story in these two ways. The conclusions, however, are not intended to satisfy us as much as to provoke us to enter into the world of this novel's first readers, who undoubtedly pondered alternate plot turns and endings with each installment.

Perhaps the most important contribution that these editors make is the thorough, careful, and helpful material that comes with the novel. In the 1960s, readers of African American literary classics had to be content with getting a fairly accurate reprint without biographical or literary context. Today we have learned to collaborate and to incorporate the tools of several disciplines to bring to the reading public the best and most authentic rendition within the most informed and well-formed professional judgments. Andrews and Kachun provide an introduction that is an exquisite example of what today's technology and techniques can do to help us situate and appreciate literature for itself and for what it represents. They have carefully researched Julia Collins, found other publications by Collins, compared her work with other writing of her time, and explained to us its potential implications. Looking at the history of the *Christian Recorder*, touching upon the rediscoveries of other texts from this and other sources, using the best data and most developed theoretical methods to speculate upon what it all means, they offer us a two-fold experience: a good story and some good information. The introduction is a marvel of information that anticipates, even when they cannot yet answer, virtually every question we might have about the text, its author, and its publication. And it is written in clear accessible language that makes a story almost as compelling as that it introduces.

I intend to use this volume as a primer for how to research early African American print culture and how to evaluate the claims made by others who present rediscovered texts. By providing us with copious notes and further references, Andrews and Kachun make it easy for us to read more and to reach farther into the past for delight and for instruction. Thanks to the Internet, microfiche and reprints of antebellum newspapers such as the *Anglo-African*, *Pacific Appeal*, *Freedom's Journal*, and *Colored American* are accessible to us all. If we pay close attention to the sources they used, the questions they asked, and the interpretations they generated, each of us can conduct her or his own quests into the *Christian Recorder* and similar resources that are now accessible. Consequently, what we have to thank these editors for is an immense opportunity as well as many minutes of reading pleasure. A lot has changed since the 1960s, and we are the fortunate beneficiaries of it all.

—Frances Smith Foster
Charles Howard Candler Professor
of English and Women's Studies
Emory University

Editors' Introduction

The Emergence of Julia C. Collins

On April 16, 1864, Julia C. Collins, a small-town schoolteacher residing in Williamsport, Pennsylvania, hitherto unknown outside her local community, issued a literary manifesto, perhaps the first by an African American woman in the United States. Collins's short essay, "Mental Improvement," appeared in the *Christian Recorder*, a weekly newspaper founded in 1852 and published in Philadelphia by the African Methodist Episcopal church.[1] The author had good reason to choose the *Recorder* for her maiden literary effort. The newspaper was not only the organ of the largest African American religious denomination in the United States; it was also the closest thing to a national newspaper that black Americans could claim as their own.

Although religious in its orientation and outlook, the *Recorder*, as Collins surely knew, did not ignore the secular world, particularly insofar as the social, political, and cultural interests of African Americans were concerned. In its "Books for Our Times" column, the *Recorder* recommended texts by black as well as white literary figures ranging from Louisa May Alcott to the fugitive-slave-turned-novelist-and-historian, William Wells Brown.[2] In keeping with its mission of uplift on all fronts, the *Recorder* nurtured and articulated a sense of racial consciousness and solidarity unbound by differences of denomination, region, and gender. A few black women, notably the early activists Frances Ellen Watkins Harper (1825–1911) and Mary Ann Shadd Cary (1823–93), found the *Recorder* a supportive forum during the first decade of the newspaper's existence. What spurred Julia Collins to send in her essay was her evident conviction that the time was right and that readers of the *Recorder* were ready to hear a black woman's call for literary agency.

"We are born with faculties and power, capable of almost anything," Collins proclaimed from the outset of her essay. "Who can measure our capacity, or set bounds to our progression in knowledge?" (121). The male editors of the *Recorder* must have been struck by the author's personal self-confidence and racial pride, asserted with an audacity reminiscent of Ralph Waldo Emerson's celebrated "American Scholar" oration of 1837.[3] To realize their intellectual potential, Collins announced, black people, irrespective of gender, needed to cultivate "the art of reading." Reading would stimulate both reflection on and creative engagement with texts, enabling readers to draw "fresh influences" and "new truths" from what they had read (122). Serious, intellectually active reading would inculcate analysis and reflection, which would in turn inspire the creativity indispensable to becoming a writer.

Having posited her reading-based notion of creativity, Collins concluded her essay with remarkable advice. "Never imitate," she urged her readers. "It is better to acquire a clear practical way of thinking for ourselves, than to load the mind with a dead weight of other men's brains." "Let us each be a 'unique,' doing cheerfully, and faithfully that which is required of us, or for which we have a particular talent; and we cannot hope too much, or dare too much" (122).

Over the next ten months Collins sent a succession of compact, often didactic essays to the *Recorder*, each one testifying to her conviction that what was required of her "particular talent" was to exercise and inspire the minds of her readers. On June 4, 1864, basking in the dawn of what she perceived as "the colored man's 'golden era'" (124), Collins chided "intelligent young girls" who "never spend one hour in trying to improve or cultivate their minds." "Our Creator never endowed us with sound minds, strong and vigorous faculties, that we should let them rest, passive and inert, for want of proper energy and ambition," Collins declared (125). Six months later Collins underlined her commitment to what she called in the title of her latest essay, "Originality of Ideas." "Originality," she observed, "is possessed by few; and why? Because we neglect self-culture, because we are too ready, too willing to depend upon the brain-work of others, till we lose our mental identity, till our originality of thought is lost in the chaos of odds and ends of other men's sentiments. We certainly have 'brain' or talent, why not use it?" (128). The pressing tone of "Originality of Ideas" carried unmistakable autobiographical implications, suggesting Collins's internal struggle to galvanize herself to bold action lest her "mental identity" be vitiated and lost.

Collins's first essay of the new year, "Life Is Earnest!," published in the January 7, 1865, issue of the *Recorder*, bore a sense of heightened urgency. "The old year has been fraught with real and important changes and events—events that have far towered—changing the seemingly invincible destiny of our people, and building us up a nation that shall shine forth as a star on the breast of time, and be gathered into the brilliant galaxy of great nations! There is a vast work for us to do! We have not a moment to lose! We have gone through life dreaming too long! We must become aroused, shake off the dead lethargy of inaction, and go to work in earnest!" (129). The hortatory mood of "Life Is Earnest!" sprang from a scarcely concealed personal motive, which Collins called "an inward long- ing, longing; a kind of remorseful dissatisfaction with ourselves: there is a void, and we feel it, and are vainly seeking and craving after some thing that is intangible" (129).

The fulfillment of Collins's "seeking and craving" became evi- dent only a month later. On February 18, 1865, under the headline, "SOMETHING NEW AND GOOD FOR OUR READERS," the *Christian Recorder* issued the following teaser: "Mrs. Julia C. Collins, now of Williams- port, Pennsylvania, proposes to write a narrative on the Curse of Cast [*sic*], through the columns of The Recorder, and as we go to press we have received the commencement, the first chapter, which will appear next week." As promised, on February 25, answering her own calls for literary innovation, intellectual independence, and action worthy of the momentous times in which she was liv- ing, Collins's novel, *The Curse of Caste; or The Slave Bride*, appeared in the *Christian Recorder*.

Publication of *The Curse of Caste*

The Curse of Caste is the earliest published novel by an African American woman yet to be discovered.[4] Collins's imaginative world focuses on the lives of a beautiful mixed-race mother and daughter whose opportunities for fulfillment through love and marriage are threatened by slavery and caste prejudice. Since the abolition of slavery in the United States had yet to be fully accom- plished when Collins launched *The Curse of Caste*, the author's de- cision to make her maternal heroine, Lina Tracy, a slave, whose husband must purchase her in order to free and then marry her, was timely. As the novel progressed through the spring, summer, and early fall of 1865, Collins shifted her attention to Lina's daughter, Claire, who grows up motherless and ignorant of her own racial heritage through the latter chapters of the novel. The impetus of the plot draws Claire ever closer to the discovery of her family, her identity, and her future. Although slavery does not menace Claire in the latter chapters of Collins's novel, the "curse of caste" does, particularly with regard to the young heroine's marital prospects. What Collins held in suspense for the ending of *The Curse of Caste* was whether Claire's moment of self-discovery as well as her own chance to become a bride would be overshadowed by "the curse of caste."

Few American novels have been serialized during a time of such fateful transition in U.S. history. When Collins began *The Curse of Caste*, the Confederate States of America was still fighting for its expiring life. Chapter 7 of the novel appeared on April 8, 1865, a day before Robert E. Lee surrendered the Army of Northern Virginia to Ulysses S. Grant at Appomattox, Virginia, thereby bringing the American Civil War to its effective end. A week later President Abraham Lincoln was assassinated. As Collins's novel churned along, Lincoln's vice president, Andrew Johnson, took the reins of the federal government and launched Reconstruction in the South. By the time Collins had finished thirty chapters of *The Curse of Caste*, twenty-three state legislatures had ratified the Thirteenth Amendment to the U.S. Constitution outlawing slavery. On September 23, 1865, the *Recorder* ran chapter 31 of *The Curse of Caste*, which placed Claire Tracy on the eve of the novel's climax, when she would finally meet her father and learn her parents'—and in a crucial sense, her own—identity. When readers of the *Recorder* opened the paper a week later, however, their expectation of learning how *The Curse of Caste* would conclude was frustrated. Instead of a chapter from the novel, the September 30 issue of the *Recorder* offered the following notice under the headline "CORRESPONDENT SICK": "We are sorry to inform our numerous readers that we received a letter, informing us of the illness of our correspondent of 'Curse of Caste; or Slave Bride' notoriety. We hope that her sickness is not unto death. We look forward to a speedy return of health and the continuation of her beautiful story. N.B.—Many persons are anxious to know whether this story will be published in book form. To all such persons we have only to say, that we do not know whether it is the author's intention to publish it in book form or not."

Readers of *The Curse of Caste* waited more than two months for the ending of Collins's "beautiful story." On December 16, 1865, the *Recorder* announced: "We are sorry to inform our readers that we have received a letter from Mr. S. C. Collins, informing us of the death of his estimable wife, Mrs. Julia C. Collins, authoress of 'The Curse of Cast [*sic*]; or, the Slave Bride.' She departed this life on the 25th of November last, and, as the letter says, in the full triumph of everlasting bliss. We know that many of our readers will be greatly disappointed on hearing that they are to be deprived of the pleasure of reading the balance of the beautiful story which she was writing for our paper."

The last known print reference to Collins came a week later when a *Recorder* correspondent who had recently visited Williamsport and was unaware of the newspaper's December 16 announcement of her death, wrote: "On Saturday, November 25th, Mrs. Julia C. Collins, the wife of Stephen C. Collins, departed this life after a short, but severe attack of consumption. Sister Collins was not a member of the church when taken sick, but, while she was contending with her affliction, she found Christ precious to her soul, and told, to all around her, what a dear Saviour she had found; and made all promise to meet her on 'Jordan's Stormy Banks,' where sickness, sorrow, pain, nor death are felt and feared no more. Mrs. Collins will not only be missed by her bereaved husband and motherless children, but by the public generally, as she was one of the writers for the Christian Recorder. Her last subject was the 'Slave Bride,' continued. The readers of your paper are anxious to see the end of that story."

If Collins composed an ending to *The Curse of Caste*, it did not survive her. Anxious readers notwithstanding, *The Curse of Caste* remained unfinished and unheralded outside the pages of the *Recorder*. Yet it seems hardly a coincidence that, four years after *The Curse of Caste* appeared, Frances Ellen Watkins Harper, destined to become the most famous African American woman novelist of the nineteenth century, serialized her first novel, *Minnie's Sacrifice*, in the same periodical that Julia Collins picked for her pioneering work. Nor is it merely curious that *Minnie's Sacrifice* centers on a heroine reminiscent of Collins's female protagonist, who faces a dilemma of racial identification on which Collins's novel was also predicated. Did Harper write her first novel and serialize it in the *Christian Recorder* as an act of literary homage to her predecessor? If so, by the end of 1870, at least one reader of the *Recorder* seems to have made the connection between Collins and Harper, although not in a favorable way. On December 24, 1870, the *Recorder* published a lengthy letter from James C. Embry, an AME churchman and future bishop,[5] who complained at length of the widespread and tenacious racism of whites, North and South, and of the lingering malaise of slavery among those black Americans who had "learned to despise themselves and their race." Rev. Embry was especially offended by the complicity of African American writers in the promotion of a self-debilitating attitude toward blackness. "Among our own people," the minister wrote, "it is a matter of shame, that almost all our writers who have attempted to produce a book, or write a serial in the papers, delineating the Negro's wrongs including the late 'curse of caste' have chosen their heroes from a class of persons of barely 'visible admixture' to represent the race. Away down in the future centuries, the readers of the history of our times will find in this fact alone a stronger proof of the malevolent character of the slavery which existed in this age, then [sic] in any other conceivable source of information."

However justified Embry's critique of *The Curse of Caste*, the fact that five years after its appearance a reader would single out *The Curse of Caste* by name as a key text in "delineating the Negro's wrongs" confirms the impact of Collins's novel on her chosen audience, the national readership of the *Christian Recorder*. The potentially controversial effect of *The Curse of Caste*—did this seemingly uplifting "beautiful story" mask a self-degrading message?—may have sparked other readers of the novel to debate its real purpose and influence. Unfortunately, because so few today are aware of Julia C. Collins's writing, we do not know, as yet, much about its literary, cultural, or social resonance. Scholarship on the history of African American literature is almost totally devoid of reference to Collins or her work.[6] Although several nineteenth-century novels and autobiographies serialized in African American periodicals have been recovered and reprinted in the last few decades (Harper's *Minnie's Sacrifice*, for example[7]), *The Curse of Caste* has never been published in book form until now.

This edition of Collins's writing aims to introduce both the author and her work to the ever-growing readership of African American women's fiction. This introduction to *The Curse of Caste* places the novel in its historical context to show what was original in Collins's novel and what its contribution was to the founding of African American women's fiction in the United States. While introducing the novel, the editors also provide the most detailed biographical portrait of Julia C. Collins available. The annotated edition of the novel itself concludes by presenting the two choices that Collins would likely have weighed as she contemplated the completion of her novel. Since both a happy ending and a tragic ending were possible outcomes for *The Curse of Caste*, this edition outlines both and discusses the advantages and disadvantages that each would have represented for Collins, given her sense of mission as an author. The edition concludes with a fully annotated rendition of all Collins's essays published in the *Christian Recorder*.

Reconstructing Julia C. Collins's Life and Community

Emerging from literary anonymity in the spring of 1864, Julia Collins's writing in the *Christian Recorder* testifies to the evolving ambitions of a traditional African American wife and mother who felt impelled to assert herself as a female public intellectual. Unfortunately, her stint on the public stage was so brief, and her identity was so wrapped up in her writing, that few additional records of her life and experience survive. Collins's meager imprint on the historical record calls to mind the lament of feminist author and critic Tillie Olsen in her book *Silences*, which was dedicated in part to "our silenced people, century after century of their beings consumed in the hard, everyday essential work of maintaining human life. Their art, which they still made—as their other contributions—anonymous; refused respect, recognition; lost."[8]

This silencing of female writers and artists is particularly evident in the case of African Americans. Even some of the best-known African American women from the nineteenth century are sparsely documented in the historical record. Several decades of intensive literary and historical scholarship on the lives of Sojourner Truth, Harriet Tubman, Harriet Jacobs, Frances Ellen Watkins Harper, and other key figures have provided us with important biographical portraits, but many questions remain, and significant portions of those women's biographies are based on inferences from circumstantial evidence. Individuals like Julia Collins are even less well known, and precious little of even the basic outlines of their lives has been recorded or preserved. Carla L. Peterson has correctly argued that, in attempting to reconstruct black women's lives, scholars must adopt an "approach that encourages speculation and resists closure," since, "given the lack of documentation, speculation . . . becomes the only alternative to silence, secrecy, and invisibility."[9]

Searching for Julia Collins in the historical record also reminds us that there were countless African Americans—both men and women—doing important work in their local or regional communities whose names and deeds were not widely recorded or recognized, and who remain unknown to us today. Examining the traces of Collins's life offers intriguing clues, not only about this pioneering author but also about the complex realities of life among northern African American families and communities, and about the ways in which individual community members attempted to assert their place in the world.[10]

Everything we know about Julia Collins dates from April 1864, when she was first mentioned in the *Christian Recorder*, to November 1865, when she died of "consumption" (tuberculosis). In addition to her own writings, Collins was mentioned in several letters to the *Recorder* from African American community members in Williamsport, Pennsylvania, where she resided during most of that time. Yet some of the most basic questions about her life remain unanswered. When and where was she born? Was she born free or enslaved, in the North or the South? Was she light skinned or dark? Where and how did she receive her education? We do not even know under what name she was born, since Collins was her married name. We know that she was married, but we know little about her husband. She had children, but we do not know with certainty how many, their names, ages, sexes, or anything else about them. We have only teasing hints as to what may have become of this family after Julia's death. Close readings of her writings and a few scattered references offer a tantalizing glimpse into the life and community of an educated and articulate African American woman living in a small, predominantly white northern town during the Civil War era.

The first verifiable reference to Julia Collins came in a letter in the April 16, 1864, issue of the *Recorder* from forty-four-year-old Williamsport resident Enoch Gilchrist, who had been one of the twelve founding members of the town's small AME congregation two years earlier. Despite being listed in the 1860 census merely as a laborer, Gilchrist maintained a position of respectability and prominence in Williamsport's black community until his death in 1895. He was active in Underground Railroad and Republican Party activities, remained a leader in the Bethel AME Church, was an officer in two local Masonic lodges, and served as one of Williamsport's delegates to a statewide meeting of the Pennsylvania Equal Rights League. In his 1864 letter, Gilchrist reported that the black children's "term of public school," which had closed in late March, would be reopened on April 11 by Mrs. Julia C. Collins, and would continue "for the Summer." Although Williamsport's formal school system would not provide facilities for African American education until the early 1870s, Collins may have been hired and compensated by the school board. This appears to have been the case with Enoch Gilchrist's father, Cornelius Gilchrist, who had been hired to teach black children during the 1850s. As with the elder Gilchrist, Collins would likely have made her own arrangements for renting space and purchasing supplies.[11]

Enoch Gilchrist's 1864 letter also noted that Rev. Nelson H. Turpin, the AME minister residing in Williamsport during his year's service on the regional Holidaysburg Circuit, was infusing the community with energy. Turpin's own earlier letter to the *Recorder*, written in February 1864, suggests that he indeed sought to "strengthen this branch of our Zion," perhaps in part by bringing the *Recorder* into the community. He claimed that "I only find one copy of the Recorder here," and asked for more to be sent. It is possible that contact with the minister and his wife, Amanda Turpin, brought the paper to Julia Collins's attention. Or, the "one copy" Turpin found may have been Julia's. In any event, by 1865 the paper seems to have become more of a presence, as Enoch Gilchrist was designated an official agent of the *Recorder* and authorized to collect subscriptions.[12]

The same issue of the *Recorder* that contained Gilchrist's letter also presented Julia Collins's first essay, "Mental Improvement," which she dated April 10—the day before her school classes were slated to begin. That Collins took her teaching career seriously was attested publicly barely two weeks later, when her second *Recorder* essay, "School Teaching," appeared. The tone of Collins's largely conventional comments about the responsibilities of teaching implied that perhaps some local parents did not fully appreciate the challenges she faced and the skills she possessed to help African American children in her community learn their lessons. Nevertheless, Collins painted a rather idyllic portrait of her classroom under a teacher who exercises "tact and patience," and who is "kind and gentle in [her] rule" (123). Evidently she was fulfilled by her work.[13]

The didactic note that Collins the schoolteacher generally sounded sometimes turned to impatient criticism, however, when she considered the misplaced priorities of too many of the girls and young women of her community. Her "Intelligent Women" essay hints at a certain anxiety about, even resentment toward, "*naturally* intelligent young girls, who never spend a thought but upon dress and pleasure. Who never spend one hour in trying to improve or cultivate their minds, while hour after hour, of precious time, is frittered away in idleness and gayety" (125). Perhaps the apparently contented schoolteacher already had reason to worry about her own "precious time," her health, and her future. If so, Collins at this point could see her womanly refuge only in "duty," in particular, the expectation of her culture that: "It is woman's province to make home happy, to be man's companion, at once tried and true; to be the mother, and instructor of his children" (125). "This is what every woman should prepare herself to become, and render herself worthy to fulfill the sacred office of wife and mother," Collins intoned (125). Yet her parting words to her female audience, whom she called "my dear young friends," urged not preparation for wifehood but individual self-development: "Improve your time, and you will never have cause to regret your choice"[14] (126).

Perhaps following her own advice, Julia Collins suspended her budding writing career for the next six months. Whatever she did between June and December 1864, Collins reappeared in the *Recorder* on December 2, writing not from Williamsport but from the shores of Lake Ontario and the town of Oswego, New York. In essays dated December 2, and December 23, 1864, her location was identified in the *Recorder* as Oswego; however, her earliest essay in 1865 came from Owego, a New York town just north of the Pennsylvania border. It is conceivable that Collins was in only one of these similarly named towns, and the paper misidentified her location. Alternatively, she may have stayed in Oswego during the earlier part of her travels, then stopped for a time in Owego on her way back to Williamsport, where she began sending in chapters of *The Curse of Caste* by mid-February 1865.[15] Did Collins remain in Williamsport, teaching through the summer as promised, and perhaps into the fall? When and why did she go to Oswego? Did she visit other communities in New York State or elsewhere? Did she travel alone, or did her husband and/or children, or someone else, accompany her? Might she even have traveled to Louisiana, the setting for much of *The Curse of Caste*? This is unlikely but not entirely inconceivable, since the area around New Orleans had been under U.S. military control since early 1862. If we knew where Collins went and what she did during what now seems to have been the six-months' gestational period for *The Curse of Caste*, we might have significantly more understanding of the impetus and preparation of Collins's crowning literary achievement.

There is some reason to speculate that during the six months before the appearance of *The Curse of Caste*, Julia Collins may have left Williamsport to seek a cure for, or at least to ease the symptoms of, her tuberculosis. This was a familiar practice among many middle-class whites, although men were more likely to travel for relief, while women, constrained by their domestic responsibilities and the era's gender conventions, were generally encouraged to stay at home. It would have been unusual for an African American woman to travel seeking a cure. Collins's tuberculosis raises still more questions about her life. This highly communicable disease might strike anyone, but it often claimed the poor and the young. Sometimes symptoms advanced very rapidly, as was the case with a fourteen-year-old African American boy from Williamsport, Benjamin Senger (or Singer), who died from tuberculosis in November 1864, "after an illness of a few weeks"; his brother William died several weeks later. In other cases the disease might lie dormant for many years, and even when active, often worked slowly to "consume" the life of the sufferer over a long period.[16] A twenty-six-year-old black Civil War veteran named Hannable Collins Bryan, from nearby Jersey Shore, Pennsylvania, died "after a lingering illness of consumption" in the spring of 1866.[17] We are told that Julia Collins died in November 1865 after "a short, but severe attack" of the disease. Given the contagious nature of tuberculosis, it is possible that Collins may have had contact with at least one of these other victims, especially since Benjamin Senger might well have been one of her students. On the other hand, she may have contracted the disease long before, and only begun experiencing renewed symptoms shortly before her death.

Also unclear is Collins's relationship to the small black community in Williamsport and the surrounding Lycoming County. By 1860 the Borough of Williamsport was a prosperous lumber center with 5,664 inhabitants, conveniently positioned on the West Branch of the Susquehanna River and well connected to other communities by rail. During the 1860s the local lumber industry boomed and the county's population grew from 37,399 to 47,626. Williamsport itself grew even more dramatically, being incorporated as a city in 1866 and reaching a population of more than 16,000 by 1870. While it remained a staunchly Democratic region politically, there was significant antislavery sentiment in Lycoming County, and both whites and blacks appear to have been involved with the Underground Railroad. The black population was small, with only about 400 in the county in 1860, among whom approximately 170 lived in Williamsport, representing 1 percent and 3 percent of those respective populations. By 1870, 851 African Americans lived in the county, with 602 in Williamsport. The overwhelming majority of blacks in Williamsport and the surrounding county were servants or laborers on farms or in the lumber industry, while some were employed as bellmen or waiters in local hotels or restaurants. A rare few had skilled trade positions as blacksmiths, barbers, shoemakers, and the like.[18]

Wherever the community's erstwhile schoolteacher Julia Collins was during those six months of silence in late 1864, during her absence from Williamsport, another African American woman there—the minister's wife, Amanda Turpin—began sending short essays to the *Christian Recorder*. Turpin's two brief essays, appearing in August 1864, each addressed what would have been considered a gender-appropriate topic: "The Character of a Wife" and "Female Influence." Both seem to support an even more subservient role for women than Collins had envisioned in her earlier "Intelligent Women" essay. Turpin's pieces are short and unremarkable,

but they suggest that there must have been some relationship between two articulate black women writing to the same newspaper
from the same small community of only a few hundred black resi-
dents. A connection between Collins and Turpin is further suggested by the fact that Turpin also became a schoolteacher by
September 1865 after her husband was reassigned to Salem, New
Jersey. Was this an intimate friendship? A bitter rivalry? Given Julia
Collins's absence, and possibly that of her husband and family,
should we read any meaning into Amanda Turpin's pondering in
her second essay: "why is it that strong men—men of intellect,
power, and talent, should be influenced or persuaded by the female to abandon one project or scheme, and repair to another?—to
flee from one city to another?"[19]

Perhaps the Turpins and the Collinses became close friends in
Williamsport. Then again, Nelson Turpin may have been less than
pleased that Julia Collins was not a member of his Bethel AME
congregation. The statement of Williamsport's circuit minister John
H. Spriggs, who had replaced Turpin sometime after April 1865,
that Collins had not been "a member of the church when taken
sick" is probably the most striking evidence we have of a distinctly
individualistic, nonconformist streak in Collins, who seems in most
other respects quite the traditional wife, mother, and schoolteacher.
Whether Collins's absence from the church rolls signaled religious
doubt, resistance to Rev. Turpin's authority, or an independence of
mind that sprang from some other source, this decision must have
been common knowledge in her community and likely a matter of
discussion, if not outright disapproval in some circles. Yet nothing
in Collins's writing indicates any specific objections to the brand
of evangelical Christianity that African American believers in
Williamsport would likely have taken for granted.

Perhaps Collins declined to join her local church because it did
not offer her the kind of opportunity for self-expression that writ-

ing for the *Christian Recorder* represented. The *Recorder* meant more to Collins than simply a way to be heard outside of Williamsport's small black community. The newspaper also gave her a way to proselytize her gospel of educational uplift and intellectual self-improvement within her Williamsport world. In February 1865, the same month *The Curse of Caste* began to appear, "Mrs. J. C. Collins" of Williamsport paid a $2.50 subscription fee to the *Recorder* on behalf of "Chas. O. Bryan." This suggests another possible community connection for Julia, since a four-year-old named Charles Bryan was listed in the 1860 census for Jersey Shore in the same household as the Hannable Collins Bryan who died of tuberculosis in 1866. Julia's connection with this family is not clear, but the coincidence of Hannable's middle name and Julia's apparent association with the younger Charles suggest that this may have been more than a casual acquaintance.[20]

Since Collins left so few traces of her life, we can only speculate about her friends and community ties in Williamsport. It is not clear whether she had lived in Williamsport for any length of time before April 1864, or where she might have lived previously. According to the 1860 federal census, the only African American "Julia" living in Lycoming County who may have been the future novelist was a literate, seventeen-year-old "mulatto" named Julia Green, who was living in the Williamsport household of Enoch Gilchrist. Julia Green does not appear in any other Williamsport sources before or after the 1860 census. Her presence in the Gilchrist household, along with twenty-seven-year-old John Green and twenty-year-old Mercey Green, is consistent with patterns of boarding within African American communities. One frequently finds individuals with surnames different from that of the household head, suggesting a pattern of taking in extended family members, orphans, children from impoverished families, or young adults in need of lodging as they attempted to establish themselves in a new community. It is not clear into which category the Greens in the Gilchrist household fell. John Green might possibly have been married to either Mercey or Julia, but it seems likely that they were siblings. It is conceivable, then, that Julia Green did become Julia Collins through marriage between 1860 and 1864, although that would make her a rather precocious twenty-one-year-old to have authored the early essays, and a rare talent to have produced *The Curse of Caste* at twenty-two. One also must wonder why she did not become Julia G. Collins after her marriage.[21]

Given the gendered biases in historical documentation, it is not surprising that Julia Collins's husband seems to have left a more accessible paper trail than his accomplished wife, albeit one that contains its share of twists, turns, and dead ends. Julia's husband first appeared in print sources when the *Recorder* reported having "received a letter from Mr. S. C. Collins, informing us of the death of his estimable wife, Mrs. Julia C. Collins." A week later the Rev. John H. Spriggs wrote his letter describing Julia's death, and identifying her as "the wife of Stephen C. Collins."[22] The next local reference to Mr. Collins appears in 1871, when a "Steve Collins" is listed in the Williamsport City Directory as a barber living in a boarding house in the African American section of the town.[23] Stephen C. Collins's whereabouts between 1865 and 1871 are not known, but he appears to have lived in Williamsport throughout the 1870s. An "S. S. Collins" authored a brief letter to the *Recorder* in 1874, reporting on the progress of Williamsport's Bethel AME Church, and an "S. C. Collins" was listed as an elected officer of a local African American Masonic lodge through 1883.[24]

Neither the 1870 nor the 1880 censuses, however, list Collins as living in Williamsport. The 1880 census does identify a forty-seven-year-old mulatto barber named "Steven Collins" living in Bloomsburg, Pennsylvania, about thirty-five miles southeast of Williamsport and easily accessible by railroad. Collins was living with his wife, a thirty-year-old mulatto named Lucretia, their six children, and two boarders. Their eldest child, an eleven-year-old son named Napoleon, was born in 1869, suggesting that his father could be the same Stephen Collins whose wife Julia had died in 1865, a supposition further supported in the name of Stephen and Lucretia's next child—a daughter named Julia, born in 1872. Bloomsburg's Steven Collins is also mentioned in an 1880 *Christian Recorder* article, which identifies him as attending a regional AME Sunday School convention in nearby Bellefonte, Pennsylvania, where he was elected president of the following year's meeting, which would take place in Williamsport. Collins's continuing ties to Williamsport are further suggested by his purchase of a plot in the city's Wildwood Cemetery in 1883. There is evidence that African Americans named Stephen C. Collins and Simon C. Collins—another African American who worked as a barber in Williamsport during the 1880s—served in the Civil War, but evidence connecting either of these men to Julia Collins is circumstantial.[25]

The search for information about Julia Collins's children is similarly confounding. It seems that she had at least two children, based on John Spriggs's reference to "her bereaved husband and motherless children."[26] The phrasing suggests that the children were relatively young, still in need of a mother's care. This, in addition to the cause of Collins's death—tuberculosis, a disease that often claimed young people during this period—permits the speculation that Collins may have been relatively young, perhaps in her thirties or even her mid-twenties, as would have been the Julia Green in the Gilchrist household in 1860. Evidence for one possible child of Julia's and Stephen's appears in the 1870 census for Williamsport with an eight-year-old mulatto named Emma Collins listed as a daughter in the household of fifty-two-year-old Simon

Floyd and his wife Julia, forty-eight. Emma would have been born around 1862 and thus could well have been Julia Collins's orphaned daughter, taken in by members of the community. The Floyds also boarded nine male laborers, a washerwoman, and a barber, all African American. While the census taker in 1870 did not list addresses, the one in 1880 was more thorough, listing the Floyd's boarding house at 122 Mill Street, next door to the boarding house at 124 Mill where Stephen Collins lived between 1871 and 1876, and where Simon C. Collins lived in 1885. Oddly, the Floyds' daughter in the 1880 census is named Anne Collins, not Emma, though the seventeen-year-old would be the right age to have been Emma in 1870. More significant still, she would also be the right age to be the "Annie Collins" who was buried in Stephen C. Collins's Wildwood Cemetery plot in 1889. Another probable daughter, Sadie Collins, is mentioned as traveling to Williamsport from Harrisburg, Pennsylvania, in February 1884, to attend "the funeral of her stepmother," Stephen's wife Lucretia Collins, who had recently died of tuberculosis.[27]

All the available evidence—both concrete and circumstantial—indicates that Julia C. Collins and her husband occupied respected positions in the community, at least for the period after 1864. They were literate, held highly prized skilled occupations, and seem to have been closely connected with the community's most well-established individuals and institutions. The many questions that remain beg further investigation, and, more broadly, suggest the extent to which the kinds of silences to which both Tillie Olson and Carla L. Peterson alluded continue to cloud our view into the past. Constructing a thorough understanding of African American community life during the mid- to late-nineteenth century—even regarding the activities of a community's most notable members—remains an enormous interpretive challenge.

Julia Collins's Literary Mission

Though additional research may reveal more about the author of *The Curse of Caste*, her family, and the community in which she lived, one thing is clear enough. Julia C. Collins was a publicly self-identified African American woman who launched her unprecedented literary career out of a strong sense of mission. Penning a series of didactic essays designed for publication in a national black newspaper was the best way this female literary unknown could garner and inform the kind of audience she needed, one that would be receptive to Collins's boldest expression of her mission—the novel taking shape in her mind.

Collins's essays articulate her affinity with key elements of what is often termed "classical black nationalism," which reached its high-water mark in the United States in the 1850s.[28] A well-read and racially conscious woman, Collins's nationalism was primarily cultural in emphasis and scope. In "Life Is Earnest!," she heralded "the seemingly invincible destiny of our people . . . that shall shine forth as a star on the breast of time, and be gathered into the brilliant galaxy of great nations!" (129). The "great nation" that Collins prophesied for black Americans was less a matter of corporate or constitutional status (she showed no sympathy for the separatist strain of black nationalism) than of cultural, in particular literary, achievement. Hence her challenges from the outset of her essays, especially to black women, in favor of "improvement of the mind, . . . cultivation and purity of taste, and the acquisition of knowledge" (122) via serious reading. Consistent with the thinking of the mid-century black middle-class, which adapted black nationalist rhetoric to advance its own socio-cultural agenda,[29] Collins advocated distinctive black cultural expression in order to reinforce racial identity and pride. Her novel as well as her essays exemplified what she hoped to elicit from her readers—a creativity that would arouse African American cultural pride and purpose, thereby promoting the process by which those whom Collins proudly called "our people" could make the historic transition into a newly empowered national consciousness.

Collins's nationalist consciousness endowed her mission as advisor to and spokesperson for black people with considerable optimism. Her essay, "Intelligent Women," composed in what she called the dawn of the colored man's "golden era," enthused: "the time is coming, with giant strides, when the black man will have only to assert his equality with the white, to have it fully and cordially awarded to him" (124–25). Yet she did not assume that all barriers were soon to fall, especially for black women. Thus she entreated her female readers to "listen to the advice of one who is closely allied with you by caste and misfortune" (126). Whether the misfortune she alluded to was the product of her personal experience of caste Collins never made clear in her writing. More discernible than any specific target of protest that may have impelled Collins's literary mission is the linkage in her mind between what God wanted her to do as a writer and what God wanted her people to become as a nation. On the eve of what would prove to be the last year of her life, Collins disclosed in "Life Is Earnest!" a rare hint of personal anxiety about her earthly career, only to deflect it by confidently anticipating her people's glorious ascent to the pinnacle of liberty. In her January 7, 1865, essay, Collins redeemed her sense of the tentativeness of life (perhaps she already knew of her illness), along with her worries about what she had done with her God-given "time and talent" by references to her sense of the "divine will" working itself out in both her individual coming-to-consciousness as a writer and her people's coming-to-consciousness as an emancipated nation. "We have been spared another year, perhaps, to improve the time and talent God has given us, working out his divine will; for it is the will of God that we become a nation and a people; and He is bringing us out of the 'depths' to the dazzling heights of liberty, where the very air is resonant with freedom" (130).

During the first half of the nineteenth century, black women preachers such as Jarena Lee (1783–?) and Zilpha Elaw (ca. 1790–?) had felt sufficiently emboldened by their faith and sense of God-given mission to author unprecedented autobiographies account-ing for their individual sense of spiritual calling.[30] But Julia Collins was the first black woman writer to suggest publicly that God's "divine will" had called her to be a novelist, indeed a novelist with a special role to play in the liberation of "a nation and a people." The last line of "Life Is Earnest!"—"it is incumbent upon us that we live for some noble purpose, some object worthy of our efforts" (130)—justifies the conclusion that, in Collins's own eyes, the "noble purpose" that awaited her in 1865 was nothing less than authoring the first African American woman's novel.

Julia C. Collins and Her Black Female Literary Contemporaries

A little more than five years before Collins began writing *The Curse of Caste*, a widowed, formerly indentured African American ser-vant named Harriet Wilson (1825–1900) hired a Boston job printer to publish a narrative that she titled *Our Nig; or Sketches from the Life of a Free Black, in a Two-Story White House, North* (1859). Had Collins known about Wilson's novelized autobiography, the Penn-sylvania housewife-turned-author might have written differently about the kind of literary "unique" she aspired to be. But given the three-hundred-mile distance separating Wilson and Collins and the extremely limited circulation of *Our Nig*,[31] we have good rea-son to doubt whether Julia Collins ever heard of Harriet Wilson or her book. Insofar as Collins and the vast majority of her readers were aware, when the *Christian Recorder* began publishing *The Curse of Caste*, its author was doing something unprecedented—writing the first African American woman's novel.

A race-conscious, uplift-minded African American woman like Collins was more likely to have heard about the pioneering personal narratives of Sojourner Truth (ca. 1797–1883) and Harriet Jacobs (1813–97) than of Harriet Wilson. While the *Narrative of Sojourner Truth* (1850) and Jacobs's *Incidents in the Life of a Slave Girl* (1861) received positive reviews from the antislavery press, Wilson's experiment in self-publication attracted no attention from the press at all. No evidence exists of a single published review of *Our Nig*, which underscores further the likelihood that Collins embarked on her novel unaware of the existence of Wilson's book.

The life stories of Truth, Wilson, and Jacobs were foundational to the creation of a self-conscious African American women's tradition in literature. It would have been hard for someone as well-informed as Julia Collins to overlook Sojourner Truth, a widely traveled, self-anointed itinerant preacher, reformer, and antislavery activist,[32] although whether Collins ever read Truth's 1850 autobiography (or any of the three reprints of it that came out later in the decade) is unknown. Determined to be heard, both Truth and Jacobs, a fugitive slave from eastern North Carolina, solicited the help of influential white female reformers to help them get their autobiographies into print.[33] Another Boston-based self-publishing venture like Truth's *Narrative* and Wilson's *Our Nig*, Jacobs's *Incidents in the Life of a Slave Girl* became well enough known to receive a comment in the *Christian Recorder*, which stated in its January 11, 1862, issue that the book had been "put into our hands by the author, Mrs. Jacobs, of New York, a colored lady, who was born a slave in North Carolina, but managed so as to wend her way to the so-called Free States." If Julia Collins subscribed to the *Recorder* just two years before she began to publish in it herself, she may have heeded the recommendation of the *Recorder's* editors and secured a copy of Jacobs's book. If any contemporary black woman writer inspired Collins, almost certainly it was the resolute example of Jacobs, herself a literary "unique" in the genre of black women's autobiography. Yet the fact that there is almost no similarity between *The Curse of Caste* and the slave narratives of Jacobs (or Truth)—other than the fact that "Linda," the pseudonymous narrator of *Incidents*, might be referred to as a light-skinned African American woman, as are the two central characters of *The Curse of Caste*—suggests that Collins's dedication to "originality of ideas" demanded that she go her own way as a novelist, rather than an autobiographer.

Publication of *The Curse of Caste* proved Collins "a unique" in African American women's literature in at least two crucial respects. First, *The Curse of Caste*, unlike the narratives of Truth, Wilson, and Jacobs, was no self-publishing venture. In keeping with its author's nationalistic cultural politics, Collins published her novel in a leading, probably *the* leading, black-operated periodical of the time.[34] Instead of Wilson's near-desperate, self-financed gamble for the attention of an indifferent public, Collins's publishing partnership with the *Christian Recorder* assured her literary venture of reaching a significant African American readership.[35] While *Our Nig*, like almost every mid-century African American autobiography, was packaged with a prefatory plea for support and appended endorsements of the author's character supplied by white people,[36] the *Christian Recorder* published Collins's novel *as* a novel without any special pleading to its readers or attempts to curry favor for its author apart from what the text could earn for itself. In an era when few black writers were able to get a hearing without first securing influential white sponsors, Collins's decision to publish in a major *black* venue, so as to reach an extensive *black* audience, signaled her commitment to an African American women's fiction that would speak to the needs and aspirations of a black readership. Publishing in the *Recorder* also ensured for *The Curse of Caste* the implicit imprimatur of the most prestigious institution in black America at the time—the African Methodist Episcopal church. A new novelist who sought the ear of black America, as Collins clearly did, could hardly have done better than to select the *Christian Recorder* as the publisher of what she believed was the first African American woman's novel.

A second reason why *The Curse of Caste* was wholly innovative stems from the fact that it is, quite plainly, a novel. Unlike every narrative by a black American woman before her, including *Our Nig*, Collins's *The Curse of Caste* emanated almost certainly from the author's own imagination, not from her autobiography. What we know about her life reveals no correspondence between Collin's biography and the people and events of *The Curse of Caste*. Collins's much-cherished ideal of originality may well have spurred the kind of imaginative license that allowed her, more than any African American novelist—male or female—before her, to declare full independence from autobiography.[37]

By contrast, *Our Nig*, although often labeled the first African American woman's novel, is, as many scholars have pointed out, essentially the story of Harriet Wilson's life. In fact, the autobiographical basis of *Our Nig* has been so thoroughly excavated by scholars and researchers in the last fifteen years that the foremost expert on Wilson's life claims that *Our Nig* "so closely corresponds to the historical record" that the book deserves to be counted as the only autobiographical narrative we have of a northern black indentured servant before the Civil War.[38]

Experimentation with fictionalizing techniques marks both *Our Nig* and *Incidents in the Life of a Slave Girl* as remarkable hybrid texts, autobiographies straining against the limits of genre and convention to tell the stories of two women hitherto silenced. *The*

Curse of Caste, on the other hand, is the first published story authored by a black American woman to set itself free of the obligation of autobiography, as far as we can tell, so as to imagine an expanded set of opportunities and a more fulfilling social reality for mid-nineteenth-century American women of color than is depicted in any previous narrative by a black American woman.

Writing a novel allowed Julia Collins to make an audacious choice, which she then passed on to the mother and daughter protagonists of her novel: the freedom to imagine and pursue in an America where slavery still existed a degree of personal fulfillment and social validation that neither Truth, Jacobs, nor Wilson could have ever thought possible, given their life experiences. That the product of Collins's imagination struck a responsive chord with her black readership is clear enough from the fact that the editors of the *Christian Recorder* acknowledged their disappointment over the lapse of *The Curse of Caste*, while at least one correspondent lamented the premature end of her "beautiful story."

The only other narrative that can vie with *The Curse of Caste* for imaginative primacy in African American women's letters is *The Bondwoman's Narrative* (2002), published from a manuscript dating probably from the mid-nineteenth century and signed by an enigmatic figure identified on the manuscript's title page as "Hannah Crafts, A Fugitive Slave Recently Escaped from North Carolina." Restored and brilliantly edited by Henry Louis Gates, Jr., *The Bondwoman's Narrative* was published with a subtitle, *A Novel* (which appears on the dust jacket of the first edition, though not on the title page), reflecting the editor's conviction that, whoever "Hannah Crafts" was, the author's aim was to write "the first novel by a female fugitive slave, and perhaps the first novel written by any black woman at all."[39] On the other hand, the noted African American scholar Dorothy Porter, who first acquired the manuscript in 1948, called it a "fictionalized biography" and "a fictionalized personal narrative," not a novel.[40] Speculation about the purposes and politics of *The Curse of Caste* and *The Bondwoman's Narrative* is inviting, but the significance of the latter text to the founding of the African American women's novel is clouded by the lingering uncertainty about the identity of Hannah Crafts. Although many hints in *The Bondwoman's Narrative* suggest that its author may well have been an African American woman, no one has effectively confirmed the racial or gender identity of the author of *The Bondwoman's Narrative*.[41] By contrast, the evidence demonstrating that Julia Collins was an African American woman is as indisputable as that which identifies Truth, Jacobs, and Wilson as Collins's black literary cohort. Thus *The Curse of Caste* demands our attention as the first serialized novel by an African American woman and the first non-autobiographical novel authored by a historically verifiable African American woman.

The Plot of *The Curse of Caste*

Although Collins's method of telling her story does not follow a strictly chronological line, this is a précis of *The Curse of Caste*:

Sometime during the slavery era in the United States, a young man from New Orleans, Richard Tracy, falls in love with a beautiful young woman he meets on a Mississippi riverboat. The woman, Lina, who does not know she is a "quadroon" and a slave, is purchased by Richard's father, Colonel Frank Tracy, a well-to-do slave owner. When Richard discovers that his betrothed is a slave in his father's possession, he enlists his friend, George Manville, to purchase Lina. The couple decamps to Connecticut where they wed and live happily for six months. Unaware that his wife has become pregnant, Richard decides to return to his family home in New Orleans to settle accounts with his irascible father.

In no mood to forgive his son, Colonel Tracy not only disinherits him but, in a rage over Richard's refusal to disavow his once-enslaved wife or his antislavery views, shoots him. While nursed back to health by Manville, Richard dictates a letter to be sent to Lina, but Manville burns the letter. Traveling to Connecticut, Manville learns of Lina's death in childbirth; entrusts the baby, Claire, to Juno Hays, a capable black nurse; and informs Richard in a letter that his wife and infant daughter are dead. Juno raises Claire to adulthood, with financial help from Manville, but the nurse never discloses to Claire the true story of her parentage and birth.

Graduating from a female seminary in the North, the beautiful and accomplished Claire Neville resolves to take a governess position in the home of a prominent New Orleans family—which happens to be that of her grandfather, Colonel Tracy. Claire's winning personality and musical talents arouse the jealousy of Isabelle, the marriageable daughter in the Tracy family, while attracting the attentions of Count Sayvord, a visiting French nobleman. Struck by Claire's resemblance to his estranged son, Colonel Tracy is moved to reconciliation with Richard. The Count, knowing that Richard has been living in France with his uncle and sensing that Claire is Richard's daughter, informs his uncle of the Tracy family mystery, which induces Richard to return to the United States.

Visiting first his former home in Connecticut, Richard learns that his daughter is alive and prepares to go to New Orleans to meet her. Meanwhile, Dr. Singleton, a friend of Colonel Tracy, conveys to Count Sayvord, who desires to marry Claire, the knowledge that Claire herself still does not possess as to the racial identity of her mother. Certain that Claire is his granddaughter by Richard and Lina, Colonel Tracy longs to welcome his son with open arms. In the last chapter of the novel, Claire anxiously awaits her father's appearance at the Tracy home.

The Curse of Caste and the Image of the Mixed-Race Woman

Even a cursory overview of *The Curse of Caste* suggests that central
to its author's purpose was the portrayal of African American women
as respectable and desirable marriage partners and as responsible
and loving mothers. Although most readers of early African American literature now recognize the importance of positive portrayal
of mothers and motherhood to the politics of early black women's
writing, it may be a bit more difficult for twenty-first-century readers to appreciate the immense sociopolitical significance that marriage rights, especially for African American women, held in the
minds of the founders of African American fiction. Yet, as the critic
Ann duCille has argued, if "modern minds are inclined to view
marriage as an oppressive, self-limiting institution, for nineteenth-
century African Americans, recently released from slavery and its
dramatic disruption of marital and family life, marriage rites were
a long-denied basic human right—signs of liberation and entitle-
ment to both democracy and desire."[42] Such a view of marriage
almost certainly motivated the author of *The Curse of Caste* in constructing the dual marriage plot of her novel. In this regard she
implicitly endorsed the claim of her African American literary predecessor, William Wells Brown, who stated in the opening para-
graphs of his pioneering novel, *Clotel; or, The President's Daughter*
(1853), that "Marriage is, indeed, the first and most important institution of human existence—the foundation of all civilization and
culture . . . and for many persons the only relation in which they
feel the true sentiments of humanity." Yet, Brown insisted, "The
marriage relation, the oldest and most sacred institution given to
man by his Creator, is unknown and unrecognized in the slave
laws of the United States."[43] No wonder, then, that Collins's novel
endorses unequivocally the freedom and fitness of African American women, whether formerly enslaved or freeborn, to marry

whom they love, regardless of actual laws forbidding slaves (such as Lina) marriage rights or caste-bound customs that would proscribe women of color (such as Claire) the same rights.

To combat the pervasive mid-nineteenth-century stereotyping of African American women, Collins evidently agreed with Brown that portraying such women in heartfelt marriages would both convey the capacity of the African American woman to "feel the true sentiments of humanity" and compel any reader of *The Curse of Caste* to feel similar "true sentiments" toward the humanity of these women. The figures with whom Collins wanted her readers most to sympathize were, of course, the beautiful mixed-race mother and daughter, Lina and Claire Neville Tracy. Perhaps out of a desire for a counterbalance to her genteel light-skinned heroines, Collins also includes in her story a wise and sustaining black nurse, Juno Hays, on whom several of the white characters, not to mention Lina and Claire, depend for key information. The repository of many Tracy family secrets, the self-sufficient and often prescient Juno is in some ways the most original character in Collins's novel. Her rock-solid marriage to a loyal, supportive, and prosperous black man provides what may be considered Collins's model of successful and lasting matrimony in *The Curse of Caste*. By naming Juno after the Roman goddess who protected women and defended marriage, Collins signified the importance of Juno to Lina and Claire, who exercise limited control of their own fates and who sometimes know less about their own identities than does Juno herself. Nevertheless, although Juno's faith in God and steadfast confidence in the eventual triumph of right offset the malignancy of the novel's two white antagonists, George Manville and Isabelle Tracy, the women who must contend with "the curse of caste" in Collins's novel are Lina and Claire, not Juno. Because Collins allows Juno to marry and live relatively unthreatened by color prejudice (although the novel suggests Juno was once enslaved), the key

questions that *The Curse of Caste* raises about the nature and fate of
African American women pertain primarily to the mixed-race heroines, Lina and Claire.

While scholars will likely find hints in *The Curse of Caste* as to
Collins's reading of British fiction from the Brontës to Dickens, the
author seems to have been influenced more by popular sentimental women's fiction in the United States and by the emerging literary presentation of the mixed-blood, or mulatta, figure in American
writing.[44] We cannot prove that Collins read mid-century race fiction by her white or black contemporaries, but it seems more than
coincidental that both Lina Tracy and her daughter Claire are represented in ways that had become, by 1865, fairly formulaic, if not
stereotypical, for mixed-race female characters in American fiction.
In the roughly ten American novels that represent the mulatta before *The Curse of Caste,* most often she is depicted as: (1) young and
beautiful with only a trace of noticeable African heritage; (2) having been raised as a white person, often of high class; (3) unaware
of her racial heritage; and (4) radically unprepared for the news
that she is actually a slave.

Once her racial identity is revealed, the fate of the mulatta, as it
works itself out in the earliest American novels to treat this character, repeatedly flirts with tragedy, which helps to explain why a
figure who bears this cross of blood came to be labeled as the "tragic
mulatta" or "tragic mulatto." Relatively few mixed-race characters appear in pre–Civil War American writing, in contrast to their
steadily growing population in post–Civil War fiction. But the tragic
destiny of Cora Munro in James Fenimore Cooper's classic
Leatherstocking novel, *The Last of the Mohicans* (1826), marked the
popular beginning of what became by the end of the nineteenth century the familiar expectation that an African American woman—no
matter how slight the admixture of color might be in her appearance or family history—could not find fulfillment or happiness in

the white world. Indeed, by the end of the century the penalty for mulattas who tried to cross the color line was generally rejection in love and social disgrace, if not death.

What is remarkable though not always acknowledged in discussions of the fate of the mulatta/mulatto in nineteenth-century American fiction is the fact that the majority of beautiful mulattas in American novels before 1865, most of which were authored by whites, do not end up unfulfilled. The most famous mulatta in antebellum American literature is Cassy in Harriet Beecher Stowe's *Uncle Tom's Cabin* (1852). Unveiled late in the novel as the desperate, hard-drinking concubine of the beastly slave owner, Simon Legree, Cassy seems a prime candidate for tragedy. But Stowe instead has Cassy engineer an escape from Legree for herself and another beautiful mulatta slated to become Legree's next sexual victim. Cassy's ultimate fate—she is reunited with her daughter Eliza, who has married the novel's mixed-race hero George Harris—restores her to her family in freedom and redeems her from the demoralization and despair that she knew in slavery.

Before 1865 most mulattas in American fiction must endure a stint in slavery and withstand intimidation by lascivious slave owners and brutal overseers, but more often than not these women eventually encounter a northerner or a European on whose love they can rely.[45] Only in *post*–Civil War American fiction does mixed-race beauty become, with increasing inevitability, the stamp of tragedy.[46] Only in postslavery America, with its hardening lines of racial separation and its mounting hysteria over white supremacy, does the mulatta/mulatto become a byword for the fear of racial pollution that many prominent white American writers pandered to or (sometimes) interrogated. Appearing in 1865 on the cusp of the new era of emancipation, *The Curse of Caste* looks back to a literary trend that, according to critics such as Judith Berzon and Suzanne Bost, preferred to imagine the near-white mulatta as a virtuous innocent committed (to the death if necessary) to established ideals of chastity, Christian wifehood, and domesticity.[47] Yet, given Collins's nationalist dreams of the future, her novel may also look forward to the post–Civil War African American novel in the hands of writers like Frances Ellen Watkins Harper, whose purpose for the mixed-race woman, according to critics such as Hazel Carby and Werner Sollors, was often that of a social mediator between the races.[48]

Collins's cultural nationalism may well have led her to consult the pioneering work of her African American male literary contemporaries—namely William Wells Brown and Frank J. Webb, author of *The Garies and Their Friends* (1857). Their treatment of mixed-race women reveals a good deal of ambivalence about how to portray the mulatta's role and fate. In *Clotel* Brown allows Althesa, sister of Clotel and the daughter of Thomas Jefferson by a slave mistress, to marry a white Vermonter, who settles in New Orleans with his bride. The marriage produces two daughters, whom tragedy strikes when their parents die in a yellow fever epidemic, leaving the unprotected daughters to be summarily sold into slavery. One commits suicide, while the other is bought by a dissipated young Southerner in order to convert her into his concubine. When her honorable lover, a Frenchman, tries to rescue her, only to be shot down by her master, the mixed-race granddaughter of Thomas Jefferson dies of a broken heart.

On the other hand, elsewhere in Brown's novel the beautiful light-skinned daughter of Clotel herself manages to marry a Frenchman, Mr. Davenant, who delivers Mary from a New Orleans slave market and takes her to Europe. There Davenant dies, leaving Mary free to marry the equally light-skinned George Green, one of the African American heroes to whom Brown entrusts the conclusion of the 1853 version of *Clotel*. Does Brown prefer his light-skinned female characters to marry light-skinned men of African descent?

Do the deaths of Althesa and her daughter imply the inadvisability of marriage across the American color line? Does the marriage of Mary to Davenant the Frenchman indicate that Brown could not imagine matrimony between a European American and an African American except somewhere outside the United States? The answers to all these questions may be yes, but Brown's fascination with mixed characters often led him to send mixed messages. For instance, in a revision published in 1864 under the title *Clotelle: A Tale of the Southern States*, Brown has his beautiful light-skinned title character marry a Frenchman who takes her to Europe before dying conveniently, thereby allowing Clotelle to wed the heroic Jerome Fletcher, who is, according to the novel's narrator, "of pure African origin."[49] While on an excursion to Geneva, Clotelle discovers her long-lost slave-owning father, whom she convinces to liberate his slaves before returning to France with her husband at the close of the novel.

Did the first African American male novelist think his mixed-race heroines were better off marrying and staying in Europe, regardless of whether their spouses were white or black? If so, disposing of his heroines in this fashion forecast the decisions of many post–Civil War fiction writers, especially whites, who, when they could countenance racial intermarriage at all, seemed to feel that Europe was the only place where such an unlikely social hybrid could survive. Webb's *The Garies and Their Friends* allows a slave owner and his former slave to move to Philadelphia in order to be legally married, but soon thereafter both die at the hands of a white mob incited by the dreaded prospect of "amalgamation." Emily Garie, a surviving daughter who is light enough to pass for white, finds a dignified and loving black suitor who wins her heart. Her brother, who actively passes for white, becomes fixated emotionally on a white woman and is devastated when her father drives him away after discovering the youth's heritage. Thus for Brown and Webb, the two male African American novelists who shared with Collins an interest in the role and fate of mixed-race women, the idea of race-mixing may have been acceptable in theory, but neither Brown nor Webb seems to have viewed racial intermarriage, especially in the United States, as a preferable outcome for an African American woman. Webb's Emily Garie finds happiness by *not* following her mother's lead, that is, by not marrying a white man.

Given this background and cultural pretext to *The Curse of Caste*, perhaps the most intriguing facet of Collins's novel is how she characterizes and emplots the fates of her two mulattas, Lina Tracy and her daughter Claire. Lina, who crosses the color line to marry the son of a slave owner, might be viewed as a tragic mulatta, given her pitiable end. Moreover, in some ways her calamitous trajectory early in the story, from the privileged white ingenue who knows nothing of her nonwhite heritage to an enslaved beauty readied for the slave market, allies her to the antebellum stereotype of the mulatta as an innocent cruelly used by circumstance. However, by rescuing Lina via a marriage to the son of the man who had enslaved her, Collins converts her mixed-race heroine into the means by which Richard Tracy, scion of the Old South, can assert his antiracist as well as antislavery convictions to his outraged father, the Tracy family patriarch. In the confrontation between the Colonel and his son, Collins suggests that falling in love with Lina confirms for Richard the impossibility of his ever assuming his patrimony as a slaveholder's son. "'Lina is not responsible for her unfortunate birth and surroundings,'" Richard protests when his father denounces the mixed-race woman as "'worse than a slave.'" Lina, Richard insists, "'is pure, refined, and good, has been educated far from the contaminating influence which southern society exerts over its followers.'" "'I would not own a slave if I possessed the wealth of a Croesus,'" Richard announces to his incredulous father. "'The institution of slavery is of itself accursed, and will yet prove the fatal Nemesis of the South, for do not think that a just God will allow any people so deeply wronged to go unavenged.'"

The polarization of slaveholding patriarch and his rebellious son, galvanized by the latter's love of a mixed-race slave, suggests that, insofar as Lina is concerned, Collins was not interested in making this mulatta a figure of mediation. Lina, intentionally or not, sets father against son, initiating a crisis that soon devolves into violence when Colonel Tracy attempts to murder Richard. Richard's near-mortal wound at the hands of his own father is the most dramatic sign in the novel of the "fatal Nemesis of the South" that slavery can and will unleash. The strife between father and son also forecasts the Civil War, often described in the 1860s as an interfamilial bloodletting or a fratricidal conflict.[50] Richard survives, but not to fight again. Instead Collins sets him emotionally adrift, homeless and alienated once he learns of his wife's death during his absence. Alone and heartbroken in the North, Lina seems yet another casualty of "the fatal Nemesis of the South." Her demise, however, does not qualify her for tragic mulatta status. Neither the direct cause of her death—the machinations of George Manville—nor the indirect cause—the inability of Richard to return to her because of "the fatal Nemesis of the South"—has anything to do with Lina's race or color. Her white husband does not reject her. He simply cannot return to her because of his near-mortal wound and the refusal of his supposed friend to inform Lina of her husband's condition. Early-twenty-first-century readers may consider Lina Tracy on her deathbed much too dependent on her husband for either her own good or that of her infant daughter. But letting Lina die as she does may well have been Collins's way of underlining her heroine's utter faithfulness to her marriage vow and devotion to her husband.

That Collins's mixed-race heroine lives almost entirely for the love of her white husband might have bothered the readers of the *Christian Recorder* more if the author had not demonstrated in the story that the all-or-nothing love of the beautiful quadroon is matched by the equally self-sacrificing love of her white husband. Although Lina's caste opposite, Richard Tracy proves that he considers Lina's love worth dying for. When Colonel Tracy threatens to disinherit his son totally for marrying "'the artful wench,'" Richard refuses to bend an inch. Instead his words provoke his father into an act that almost brings about Richard's violent death. Like Lina, Richard is willing to risk all for love.

Although Collins tells us that Lina "was not a brunette, but hers was that dark brownish skin which we observe in the Spaniard and half-breed Indians," Richard never gives a moment's thought to his wife's color, nor does he fret during the time they are married about the possible color of their children. So indifferent are Lina and Richard to anxieties about color or caste that they marry without hesitation and set up housekeeping in Connecticut, where the Tracy family came from. It is significant that Collins does not have Lina and Richard debate about whether their marriage and family would be better off in Europe. In the middle of Connecticut Yankeedom the couple seems quite content, enjoying pleasant relations with Richard's aunt, whose clergyman husband had solemnized their vows. Although Collins gives her interracial couple only six months of blissful togetherness, that is quite enough to make her point, which seems to have been to portray a fulfilling marriage between a white man and a woman of acknowledged African descent taking place in an America where love, rather than color or caste, would be the determinant of the marriage's viability and success.

If we think of the cultural import of this marriage to the evangelical readership of the *Christian Recorder*, the moral of the Lina and Richard Tracy story may well have been: whom God hath joined together, let no one (white or black) put asunder. As god of her fictional universe, Collins allows two white men, the villainous Manville and the intransigent Colonel Tracy, opportunity to suppress the love or thwart the marriage of the novel's ideally devoted husband and wife. Ultimately, however, Manville on his deathbed repents of all his evil machinations, while the closing chapters of the novel show the Colonel, his heart healed of vengeance and, to some degree, of racial prejudice by the daily ministrations of his granddaughter (whose racial identity and paternity he has surmised), longing to be reunited with his son. If this was Collins's metaphor of reconciliation between the South and the North after the Civil War, the process by which the Colonel is reconstructed in the novel is well worth attention. It is striking, for instance, that the restoration of the Tracy family that seems on the verge of taking place at the end of the story is due primarily to the child of a union that the Colonel once called "accursed" but eventually refers to only as "unfortunate."

The offspring of the sacrificial love of Lina and Richard Tracy, Claire Neville plays a noticeably redemptive role in *The Curse of Caste*. Because we do not have the climactic ending of the novel, however, we cannot be sure how Claire's redemptive work would have finally evolved. But we can see that while Claire, even lighter-skinned than her mother, is every bit as beautiful, pure and refined, loving and talented, and innocent as Lina Tracy, the daughter possesses an independence of mind and purpose that does not emerge from her mother's character. While Lina's love of her husband nerves her to take the radical step of interracial marriage without, apparently, any hesitation, she lacks the independent spirit of her daughter who, after finishing her studies, resolves to move to the South and become a governess despite contrary advice from a girlhood friend and her old nurse Juno. Claire wishes to be "strong to do and dare," although it is unclear in the novel just how much she is prepared to dare and for what purpose.

Collins's *Christian Recorder* readers no doubt warmed to Claire's willingness to go to work to support herself. A well-educated and high-minded young woman consigning herself, in effect, to the servant class to help an invalid lady and her children would have made Claire all the more sympathetic, particularly when her mean stepsister foil, the proud and selfish Isabelle Tracy, enters the story. Isabelle's "hatred" toward Claire commences from the moment they meet; it only worsens as the novel proceeds. Steely, heartless, and uncontrollably jealous, albeit hauntingly beautiful, Isabelle Tracy represents almost everything the *Christian Recorder*'s female readership must have loved to hate in the stereotypical white Southern belle of the slaveholding South. She, not her brother Richard, is the chip off the old block of the paterfamilias, Colonel Tracy. While Isabelle repels everyone in the story, even Count Sayvord, whom she hopes to marry, Claire unconsciously draws everyone into her beneficent orbit. She becomes the means by which the moral regeneration and reconciliation of the Tracy family are set in motion in the novel. While Claire does none of her redemptive work with an eye to her own advantage, most readers of the *Christian Recorder* would probably have judged her an admirable instrument of God's providence and grace.

Although morally idealized, Claire is endowed with one besetting anxiety, which she articulates in the opening chapter of the novel: "'I am homeless and almost friendless—have never known a mother's kind, protecting care, and I don't know that I even have a right to the name I bear. I know nothing of my mother, not even her name.'" Discovering the identity of her mother and the circumstances of her parentage are among the most likely outcomes we can expect that Collins had in mind for the ending of *The Curse of Caste*. The plot of the novel is so constructed as to bring father and daughter inevitably back together, where, it seems certain, Richard will not only embrace Claire as his child but also tell her who her mother was.

It is possible, of course, that Collins might have had Richard decide *not* to disclose the truth of Lina's racial heritage to their daughter.[51] One remarkable feature of *The Curse of Caste* is that on the verge of its climax, the three most important men in Claire's life—her father, her grandfather, and the man who wishes to marry her—all know the secret of her racial heritage, but she doesn't. Perhaps Collins set up the climax of the novel in this way to place the moral onus for Claire's future on white men, who could either consign "the curse of caste" to her or exempt her from the curse simply by refusing to tell her of her mother's racial identity.

Nevertheless, it is difficult to believe that a writer of Collins's nationalist proclivities would have been satisfied to end her novel by allowing her heroine to remain ignorant of her mother's identity or the depth of her father's love, which transcended caste bugaboos and the violent bigotry of her grandfather. It is much more likely that Collins intended for the final chapters of her novel to picture Richard Tracy telling his daughter the whole truth about her mother. It is just as likely that Claire, relieved finally to know that her mother was the embodiment of wifely loyalty and love, would have received with equanimity the revelation of her own racial heritage. Any other reaction to this information would contradict the logic of Collins's plot, which was that America's "curse of caste" was socially enforced, not divinely appointed, and thus could be lifted and abandoned even by people as bigoted as Colonel Tracy, once they had learned to open their hearts, as the Colonel does, to forgiveness and love.

The Curse of Caste could not have ended, however, without a final scene in which the author addressed the question of Claire's marriage. Collins manages her plot so as to convert Count Sayvord, the once-presumed suitor of Isabelle, into the passionate admirer of the young governess, who is far too devoted to others to notice, let alone encourage, Sayvord's attention. One important element of suspense in the novel is whether Sayvord will propose to Claire, and if so, under what circumstances. In chapter 29, the Tracy family doctor inquires of Sayvord as to his intentions regarding Claire. The French nobleman replies, "'I do love Claire—and if she will accept me, I will make her my wife, beloved and honored above woman.'" But when the doctor informs the Count of Claire's racial ancestry and warns him that "caste" may become "the bane" of his married life even as it "proved the bane of Richard Tracy's life," Sayvord equivocates. Instead of proclaiming his undying love for Claire regardless of her racial heritage, as Richard did when his father told him of Lina's slave past, Sayvord turns noncommittal: "'I must think of this, Doctor. It is best to accustom one's self to look unpleasant facts steadily in the face; and I thank you for your forethought.'" Sayvord does not explain the "unpleasant facts" that give him pause, nor do the last chapters hint as to whether the Count will ignore caste and propose to Claire, or observe caste and forego any declaration of love.

At the end of *The Curse of Caste*, therefore, readers face three tantalizingly unresolved questions. First, will Count Sayvord, knowing Claire's racial identity, propose to her? Second, will Claire, knowing her racial identity, accept the Count's proposal, if he *does* ask her to marry him? Having refused a happy ending to the first interracial marriage in her novel, will Collins allow the unoffending offspring of that marriage to enter into marriage herself? If so, how, where, and to what end?

The answers to these questions, according to the editors' best conjecture, appear in the appendix to the following text of *The Curse of Caste*. The two conclusions appended to the text of the novel offer today's readers something that Collins's readers in 1865 never got: a chance to contemplate how her unprecedented novel could or should have ended. Regardless of how today's readers re-create the novel's conclusion for themselves, *The Curse of Caste*, so long silenced and forgotten, compellingly transposes the suspense of its unresolved ending to our own era in history when interracial marriage, though far more common than in Collins's day, remains highly controversial. How we decide that this novel might have ended in 1865 may well be a revealing indicator of how we believe the unresolved issues that Collins did not live to work out in fiction should be resolved in multiethnic America today.

Notes to Introduction

1. The best study of the early history of the *Christian Recorder* is Gilbert Anthony Williams, *The Christian Recorder, Newspaper of the African Methodist Episcopal Church: History of a Forum for Ideas, 1854–1902* (Jefferson, NC: McFarland, 1996). Founded as the *Christian Herald* in 1848, the name of the weekly changed to the *Christian Recorder* in 1852, when its publication office moved from Pittsburgh, Pennsylvania, to Philadelphia. See Daniel A. Payne, *History of the African Methodist Episcopal Church* (Nashville: AME Sunday School Union, 1891), 297–305. Collins's "Mental Improvement," *Christian Recorder* 4 (16), April 16, 1864, is reprinted, with all her other known essays, in this volume. All quotations from Collins's essays in this introduction refer to the pagination of this volume.

2. In the February 20, 1864, issue the *Recorder* notes William Wells Brown's novel *Clotelle* (1864) and Louisa May Alcott's *Hospital Sketches* as volumes in James Redpath's new series, Books for the Camp-Fires. The January 16, 1864, column "Books for the Times" recommends Brown's *The Black Man* (1863), a collection of "biographical sketches of fifty-eight distinguished colored men and women," along with a volume of the writings and speeches of the famed antislavery orator, Wendell Phillips, and a biography of the Haitian revolutionary Toussaint L'Ouverture. Other issues of the *Recorder* in 1864 list religious titles as worthy of its readers' note.

3. Ralph Waldo Emerson delivered his oration, "The American Scholar," to the Phi Beta Kappa society at Harvard University on August 31, 1837. When published in 1848, it became one of the most influential essays of its time. In the speech, Emerson called for original thinking and writing from his generation of Americans. His emphasis on "creative reading as well as creative writing" and his bold assertion that "we will walk on our own feet; we will work with our own hands; we will speak our own minds" may have helped to inspire Collins's exhortations in favor of a "mental improvement" that led to true intellectual independence and enterprise, not merely depositing in the mind the "dead weight of other men's brains." See "The American Scholar" in *The Norton Anthology of American Literature*, ed. Nina Baym et al., 6th ed. (New York: W.W. Norton, 2003), vol. B, 1135–47.

4. Although Harriet Wilson's *Our Nig; or, Sketches from the Life of a Free Black in a Two-Story White House, North* (Boston: printed privately by the author, 1859) is often called the first African American woman's novel, scholarship on this text in the last two decades has revealed that the events of *Our Nig* are based almost entirely on Wilson's own life. Many critics now regard *Our Nig* as a novelized autobiography. In the title and preface of *Our Nig*, Wilson's choice of descriptors for her book, namely "sketches" and "narrations," point to the autobiographical rather than fictional character of her book. Appended to *Our Nig* is a friend's endorsement of the author's character and veracity. "Allida" praises Wilson for "writing an Autobiography" as a means of supporting herself in a respectable fashion. See *Our Nig*, ed. P. Gabrielle Foreman and Reginald H. Pitts (New York: Penguin, 2005), 76.

5. James C. Embry (1834–97), a national figure in the AME Church, was elected bishop in 1896.

6. A notable exception is the appreciative paragraph that Dickson D. Bruce, Jr. accords *The Curse of Caste* in *The Origins of African American Literature, 1680–1865* (Charlottesville: University Press of Virginia, 2001), 306–7. *The Curse of Caste* was first reprinted on microfiche in serialized form in 1994 in *The Black Periodical Fiction Project*, ed. Henry Louis Gates, Jr. (Microfiche 2249.07–2255.03, Unit 12, Chadwyck-Healy, 1994–97).

7. Martin R. Delany's *Blake; or, The Huts of America* was serialized in the *Anglo-African Magazine*, January–July 1859 and in the *Weekly Anglo-African*, November 23, 1861–April/May 1862. Missing its final chapters, which have not yet been located, *Blake*, edited by Floyd J. Miller, was published in book form in 1970 by Beacon Press. Written in 1849 but not published until it was serialized in the Indianapolis *Freeman* in 1896, *Free Man of Color: The Autobiography of Willis Augustus Hodges* was rediscovered and edited by Willard B. Gatewood

for the University of Tennessee Press in 1982. Three serialized novels that Frances E. W. Harper published in the *Christian Recorder* (after *The Curse of Caste*) appeared for the first time in book form in *Minnie's Sacrifice, Sowing and Reaping, and Trial and Triumph: Three Rediscovered Novels by Frances E. W. Harper*, ed. Frances Smith Foster (Boston: Beacon, 1994).

8.   Tillie Olsen, *Silences* (New York: Dell Publishing, 1978).

9.   For example, Nell Irvin Painter, *Sojourner Truth: A Life, A Symbol* (New York: W. W. Norton, 1996); Catherine Clinton, *Harriet Tubman: The Road to Freedom* (New York: Little, Brown & Co., 2004); Jean Fagan Yellin, *Harriet Jacobs: A Life* (New York: Basic Books, 2003); Melba Joyce Boyd, *Discarded Legacy: Politics and Poetics in the Life of Frances E. W. Harper, 1825–1911* (Detroit: Wayne State University Press, 1994); Frances Smith Foster, *Written By Herself: Literary Production by African American Women, 1746–1892* (Bloomington: Indiana University Press, 1993). Carla L. Peterson has called attention to these biographical challenges in her insightful essay, "Subject to Speculation: Assessing the Lives of African American Women in the Nineteenth Century," in *Women's Studies in Transition: The Pursuit of Interdisciplinarity*, ed. Kate Conway-Turner, Suzanne Cherrin, Jessica Schiffman, and Kathleen Doherty Turkel (Newark: University of Delaware Press, 1998), 109–17, quoted at 116 and 114. Aside from her own writing, most of what is known about Julia Collins comes from brief and scattered references in the pages of the *Christian Recorder*. Despite concentrated research in a wide range of national, local, and regional archives, libraries, historical societies, and other repositories, very little concrete information about Julia Collins has been uncovered. Local and national newspapers; census records; birth, death, and marriage records; deeds; cemetery records; city directories; military records; and other such sources have yielded virtually no concrete references to Collins. This brief introduction summarizes the little which is known and speculates about other aspects of Julia Collins's life and social world. Our hope is that other scholars will find here a useful starting point from which to continue the search for historical documentation of Collins, her family, and her community.

10. An excellent example of historical research on a little-known nineteenth-century African American community leader, whose life is better documented than Collins's, is Nick Salvatore's *We All Got History: The Memory Books of Amos Webber* (New York: Times Books, 1996).

11. Letter from E. Gillchrist [*sic*], *Christian Recorder*, April 16, 1864; "Enoch Gilchrist Dead," undated newspaper clipping, including the handwritten note: "Died Dec. 25, 1895," in Meginnis Clipping File, Box G (mfilm) James V. Brown Library, Williamsport, Pennsylvania; "Blacks and Formal Education," typescript in the Vertical File "Blacks in Williamsport," James V. Brown Library. Gilchrist's status in the

Masonic Lodges noted in *Boyds' Williamsport City Directory*, 1871–72 (Williamsport, PA: Boyd and Boyd, 1871), 122; and in *Boyds' Williamsport City Directory*, 1873–74 (Williamsport, PA: Boyd and Boyd, 1873), 110–11. Gilchrist and Rev. John Spriggs are listed as delegates to the 1866 Annual Meeting of the State Equal Rights League in the *Christian Recorder*, August 18, 1866. *Boyds' Williamsport City Directory*, 1871–72, 115, contains the first listing of a "Colored School, ungraded" administered by the district, which was taught by "Miss Anna Watson."

12.   Letter from E. Gillchrist [*sic*], *Christian Recorder*, April 16, 1864; letter from N. H. Turpin, *Christian Recorder*, February 13, 1864. Enoch Gilchrist's position as *Recorder* agent noted in *Christian Recorder*, May 20, 1865.

13.   "School Teaching," *Christian Recorder*, May 7, 1864.

14.   "Intelligent Women," *Christian Recorder*, June 4, 1864.

15.   "A Letter from Oswego: Originality of Ideas," *Christian Recorder*, December 10, 1864; "Life is Earnest," *Christian Recorder*, January 7, 1865; "Memory and Imagination," *Christian Recorder*, January 28, 1865. The only evidence that might place her in one or the other community consists of two notations in the Oswego *Daily Commercial Advertiser* under the unclaimed letters column from the town's post office. These are suggestive, but hardly conclusive. On March 6, 1865, the list indicated an unclaimed letter for "Collins, Stephen" (the name of Julia's husband) and on August 21, 1865, one for "Collins, miss Julia C." By this time, of course, we are sure that Julia, at least, was back in Williamsport and therefore would not be receiving her mail in Oswego. But this information does not confirm that she was ever there in the first place. A reader of the *Recorder* wanting to communicate with the author would have believed she was in Oswego, based on the information supplied by the newspaper.

16.   Sheila Rothman, *Living in the Shadow of Death: Tuberculosis and the Social Experience of Illness in American History* (Baltimore: Hopkins Fulfillment Service, 1995); letter from Rev. Nelson H. Turpin, *Christian Recorder*, April 22, 1865.

17.   Letter from Joseph Bryan [dated April 14, 1866], *Christian Recorder*, April 21, 1866; "A Letter from Hollidaysburg Circuit" [from Rev. John H. Spriggs, dated December 14, 1865], *Christian Recorder*, December 23, 1865. The middle name "Collins" of the deceased veteran is, of course, eye-catching, especially since Julia Collins's name was associated with a Charles Bryan; the relationship between the families requires further investigation.

18.   Robin Van Auken and Lou Hunsinger, Jr., *Williamsport: Boomtown on the Susquehanna* (Mount Pleasant, SC: Arcadia Publishing, 2003), 29–73; *History of Lycoming County Pennsylvania*, ed. John F. Meginnis,

published in 1892, reproduced electronically and available at www.usgennet.org/usa/pa/county/lycoming/history/lyco-history-01.html,. 338–79, accessed September 20, 2005. Black population statistics for Lycoming County from Historical Census Browser, http://fisher.lib.virginia.edu/collections/stats/histcensus/php/ newlong.php, accessed September 18, 2005. Population for Williamsport from www.ancestry.com. Ralph L. Lester, "Freedom Road," *Journal of the Lycoming County Historical Society* 1.9 (June 1959), 22–23; "A Peep at the Past," *Pennsylvania Grit* (Williamsport, PA), April 14, 1901, 2; "Robert Hughes, Who Once Helped Slaves to Freedom, Dies at Family Homestead," *Williamsport Sun*, June 11, 1941; "Prominent Abolitionists," typescript, Janet Trice Collection, and "A Picture of Lycoming County," typescript, both at the Thomas E. Taber Museum, Lycoming County Historical Society; "The Underground Railroad," pamphlet, and "Slavery," typescript, both in "Blacks in Williamsport" Vertical File, James V. Brown Library.

19. "The Character of a Wife," *Christian Recorder*, August 6, 1864; "Female Influence," *Christian Recorder*, August 20, 1864; letter from Nelson Turpin, *Christian Recorder*, September 30, 1865. One might wonder what role pastor Nelson H. Turpin played in the women's relationship. Several years later, in 1869, while he was assigned to the Sullivan Street AME Church in New York City, Turpin was described as "fierce" by black evangelist and autobiographer Amanda Berry Smith. While Smith "would go to see Sister Turpin and the children," she claimed to be "afraid of Brother Turpin." If Turpin was a hard man to deal with, he seems to have supported his wife's submissions to the *Recorder*. The same issue that contained Amanda Turpin's first essay also contained a letter from her husband reporting the state of affairs in his charge, so it seems likely that they had been sent in together. See Amanda Smith, *An Autobiography: the Story of the Lord's Dealings with Mrs. Amanda Smith, the Colored Evangelist: a machine-readable transcription*, Digital Schomburg African American Women Writers of the Nineteenth Century, http://digilib.nypl.org/ dynaweb/digs-b/wwm97264/@Generic__BookView (original Chicago, 1897), 109–10, accessed October 17, 2004; and "Letter from Brother Turpin," *Christian Recorder*, August 6, 1864.

20. "Acknowledgements," *Christian Recorder*, February 25, 1865.

21. The practice of boarding in antebellum African American communities is discussed in James O. Horton and Lois E. Horton, *In Hope of Liberty: Culture, Community, and Protest Among Northern Free Blacks, 1790–1860* (New York: Oxford University Press, 1996), 96–100, 129, 289 nn65–66. The persistence of boarding in the early twentieth century has been documented by Andrea G. Hunter, "Making a Way: Strategies in Southern Urban African-American Families, 1900 and

1936," *Journal of Family History* 18:3 (1993), 231–48; Andrew Wiese, "Stubborn Diversity: A Commentary on Middle-Class Influence in Working-Class Suburbs, 1900–1940," *Journal of Urban History* 27:3 (2001), 347–54; and Kimberley L. Phillips, "'But it is a fine place to make money': Migration and African-American Families in Cleveland, 1915–1929," *Journal of Social History* 30:2 (1996), 393–413. Late-nineteenth-century African American households, extended family, and fictive kin patterns are also discussed in Elizabeth A. Regosin, *Freedom's Promise: Ex-Slave Families and Citizenship in the Age of Emancipation* (Charlottesville: University of Virginia Press, 2002).

22. "Death of Mrs. Julia C. Collins," *Christian Recorder*, December 16, 1865; "A Letter from Hollidaysburg Circuit," *Christian Recorder*, December 23, 1865.

23. *Boyds' Williamsport City Directory*, 1871–72 (Williamsport, PA: Boyd and Boyd, 1871), 142. The first city directory covering Williamsport was published in 1867, two years after Julia Collins's death.

24. The *Christian Recorder*, April 2, 1874, has a letter from "S. S. Collins" of Williamsport, which may represent a typographical error. Entries for S. C. Collins as an officer of the "St. John's Chapter (col'd) No. 40 A.Y.M." appear in the Williamsport City Directories from 1877 through 1880, although no S. C. Collins is listed in the residential section of the directories during those years.

25. 1880 U.S. Federal Census (Population Schedule), Bloomsburg, Columbia County, Pennsylvania, Roll T9_1118; Family History Film 1255118; Page 56A; Enumeration District 165; Image 0386 [Digital scan of original records in the National Archives, Washington, DC], www.ancestry.com, accessed June 6, 2005; *Christian Recorder*, August 12, 1880. Unless we are dealing with multiple African American barbers named Stephen (or Steven or Steve) Collins in these nearby communities, it seems that this man was also the same Stephen C. Collins who purchased a ten-grave burial plot in Williamsport's Wildwood Cemetery in 1883. Information provided by Michael L. Figels, Office Manager, Wildwood Cemetery Co., Williamsport, Pennsylvania, confirms that Stephen Collins and the two individuals buried there were African Americans. There is no indication of where Stephen Collins himself is buried, but apparently neither he nor Julia is in the Wildwood plot. Stephen's presumed second wife, Lucretia Collins, also appears not to have been interred in the Wildwood plot upon her death, ironically also of tuberculosis, which was reported in the *Pennsylvania Grit* (Williamsport, PA), February 16, 1884. Wildwood's records indicate that the plot remained unoccupied until 1889, when an Annie Collins, age twenty-seven, was buried there. The only other occupied grave is that of Jen L. Caulion, who was laid to rest at age forty-two in 1892. The identity of S. C.

Collins becomes more clouded with a reference to the establishment of a black Grand Army of the Republic (GAR) Post in
Williamsport in the early 1880s. The GAR was an organization for
United States Civil War veterans. In some cases African Americans
could join predominantly white posts, but black veterans often
formed separate posts—partly because they were frequently excluded from, or marginalized within, white posts, and partly to assert their own independence and community leadership. Coverage
of a regional GAR encampment in 1884 commented on the "Colonel Fribley Post No. 390, of Williamsport, under the leadership of
Commander S. C. Collins," which was "composed of colored veterans entirely." The identity of this S. C. Collins is complicated by the
presence in the 1885–86 Williamsport City Directory of a barber
named Simon C. Collins, living in the same boarding house where
the barber "Steve Collins" had lived a decade earlier. Moreover, a
Stephen S. Collins is listed as a barber in Williamsport in the City
Directories from 1889 to 1892. There is evidence of African Americans named Stephen C. Collins and Simon C. Collins having served
in the Civil War, and therefore qualifying for membership in the GAR.
Democratic Watchman (Bellefonte, PA), August 22, 1884, 4, 5. Index of
Civil War Soldiers, 1861–1866, mfilm reel 3186, Pennsylvania State
Archives. The possibility that Stephen C. and Simon C. Collins are
the same man is also suggested by separate records showing that a
man under each name enlisted as a Sergeant in Company I, Sixth
Infantry Regiment of the United States Colored Troops, with Stephen
listed as mustering out in August 1865, and Simon in September 1865.
For Stephen C. Collins, see Special Schedule—Surviving Soldiers,
Sailors, and Marines, and Widows, etc. at ancestry.com, 1890 *Veterans Schedule* [database online], (Provo, UT: My Family.com, Inc.,
2005). Original data: *Special Schedules of the Eleventh Census (1890)
Enumerating Union Veterans and Widows of Veterans of the Civil War.*
M23, 118 rolls. National Archives and Records Administration,
Washington, DC. For Simon C. Collins, see Historical Data Systems
comp. *Military Records of Individual Civil War Soldiers* [database
online], (Provo, UT: Ancestry.com, 1999–). A twenty-six-year-old
sergeant named "Simon C. Collons" (whose occupation is noted as
"barber") is listed in the transcribed muster roll of Company I in
James Paradis, *Strike the Blow for Freedom: the 6th United States Colored Infantry in the Civil War* (Shippensburg, PA, 1998), 171. It is interesting that most African Americans from Lycoming County enlisted
in the Eighth Regiment, USCT, with others in the Fourteenth Rhode
Island Heavy Artillery and Eleventh USCT Heavy Artillery. No mention of any Lycoming County Collins exists in local history sources
("Black Civil War Veterans," pamphlet, and "Black Soldiers from

Lycoming County," typescript, both in "Blacks in Williamsport" Vertical File, James V. Brown Library). The records indicate that Simon Collins mustered out in September 1865 and Stephen in August 1865. If either of these men were Julia's husband, then he was almost certainly not present in Williamsport with Julia and the children between 1863 and 1865.

26. "Death of Mrs. Julia C. Collins," *Christian Recorder*, December 16, 1865; "A Letter from Hollidaysburg Circuit" [from Rev. John H. Spriggs, dated December 14, 1865], *Christian Recorder*, December 23, 1865.

27. *Pennsylvania Grit* (Williamsport, PA), February 16, 1884. The relationships among these individuals are perplexing. Could Simon and Stephen (or Steve or Steven) be the same person, with nicknames being used interchangeably with a given name? Could the use of a nickname, and the butchered spelling of a last name, allow us to identify the Jen L. Caulion in Wildwood Cemetery as the Lucretia Collins married to Bloomsburg's Stephen Collins in 1880, and who died in 1884? Could nicknames or careless record keeping explain the relationship between Annie and Emma Collins, or the appearance of S. S. Collins? Very little scholarship exists on name changing practices among African Americans, or on the difficulties posed by name variations in censuses, city directories, and other records. One useful study on such issues in Canadian records is Christian Pouyez, Raymond Roy, and Martin François, "The Linkage of Census Name Data: Problems and Procedures," *Journal of Interdisciplinary History* 14:1 (1983): 129–52. For the Collins family, at this point the questions outnumber the answers.

28. Collins's affinity with classical black nationalism can be seen by examining Wilson Moses's standard study of the subject in *The Golden Age of Black Nationalism, 1850–1925* (New York: Oxford University Press, 1978), 27–55.

29. Collins seems to have had sympathy with the ideas of some nineteenth-century black nationalists who tried to valorize what historian Patrick Rael has called "a distinct black cultural heritage" in *Black Identity and Black Protest in the Antebellum North* (Chapel Hill: University of North Carolina Press, 2002), 210. Rael comments on the adoption of cultural nationalism by black middle-class writers, especially those who, like Collins, reinforced their own nationalism by using black newspapers to publicize their ideas. Collins's use of the *Christian Recorder* to espouse her nationalist sentiments also supports Elizabeth McHenry's argument for the critical "role of print in the formation of nationalism." Black newspapers in particular, she argues, "were crucial to the formation of an ideal of community that affirmed reading and other literary activities as acts of

public good on which the intellectual life and civic character of its members could be grounded." Elizabeth McHenry, *Forgotten Readers: Recovering the Lost History of African-American Literary Societies* (Durham, NC: Duke University Press, 2002), 87. McHenry here follows the argument presented in Benedict Anderson's *Imagined Communities: Reflections on the Origin and Spread of Nationalism* (London and New York: Verso, 1991).

30. *The Life and Religious Experience of Jarena Lee, a Coloured Lady* (1836) and *Memoirs of the Life, Religious Experience, Ministerial Travels and Labours of Mrs. Zilpha Elaw, an American Female of Colour* (1846) are reprinted in William L. Andrews, ed., *Sisters of the Spirit* (Bloomington: Indiana University Press, 1986). For informed analysis of these autobiographies, see Joycelyn Moody, *Sentimental Confessions: Spiritual Narratives of Nineteenth-Century African American Women* (Athens: University of Georgia Press, 2001); and Elizabeth Elkin Grammar, *Some Wild Visions: Autobiographies by Female Itinerant Evangelists in 19th-Century America* (New York: Oxford University Press, 2003).

31. P. Gabrielle Foreman and Reginald H. Pitts, the editors of the most recent scholarly edition of *Our Nig*, point out that the white antislavery movement "ignored" the book, while African American readers "overlooked" it as well. See *Our Nig*, ed. Foreman and Pitts, xxiv–xxv.

32. The earliest mention of Sojourner Truth in the *Christian Recorder* appeared in its "News of the Week" column on June 22, 1867, which noted Truth's arrival in Rochester, New York, accompanied by a group of ex-slaves from Virginia, for whom she was evidently seeking employment.

33. *Narrative of Sojourner Truth* (Boston: published privately by the author, 1850) was written by Olive Gilbert, a white feminist and antislavery activist whom Truth selected as her amanuensis. *Incidents in the Life of a Slave Girl* (Boston: published privately by the author, 1861) was edited by Lydia Maria Child, a well-known author of fiction and a committed abolitionist writer.

34. According to Rael, nineteenth-century black newspapers "served as the great mechanism for constructing a unified, even pan-African black identity, one that could protest the interests of the free and the slave." See Rael, *Black Identity*, 216.

35. Scholars such as Frances Smith Foster and Elizabeth McHenry have made compelling arguments about the centrality of "the Afro-Protestant press" to the creation and dissemination of African American literature in the mid-nineteenth century. Their research has convincingly demonstrated that "the Afro-Protestant press must be reconsidered as a major source of literature by and for African

Americans" (McHenry, *Forgotten Readers* 137). By failing to recognize the key role of periodicals such as the *Christian Recorder* in the founding of African American literature, Foster warns that African American literary history will remain "ahistorical" and incomplete, hampered by twentieth- and twenty-first-century notions of the discreteness of the secular and the sacred. See the introduction to Foster's *Minnie's Sacrifice, Sowing and Reaping, and Trial and Triumph: Three Rediscovered Novels by Frances E. W. Harper* and her essay, "A Narrative of the Interesting Origins and (Somewhat) Surprising Developments of African-American Print Culture," *American Literary History* (2005): 712–40.

36. Endorsements of the veracity of African American authors, either in prefatory or appended statements usually by whites, are standard features of African American autobiographies in the middle of the nineteenth century. That *Our Nig* follows this practice provides further reason to conclude that it is an autobiography, albeit fictionalized in several interesting respects. For a discussion of white-authored "authentication" documents in mid-nineteenth-century African American autobiographies, see Robert B. Stepto, *From Behind the Veil: A Study of Afro-American Narrative* (Urbana: University of Illinois Press, 1979), 6–30.

37. For a discussion of the rootedness in history and autobiography of early African American male fiction, see William L. Andrews, "The Novelization of Voice in Early African American Narrative," *PMLA* 105 (January 1990): 23–36.

38. Foreman and Pitts, *Our Nig*, xxiv. Barbara A. White, another important critic of *Our Nig*, who uncovered numerous links between the text and Wilson's life, reminds readers that Wilson never claimed *Our Nig* to be a novel. See White's "'Our Nig' and the She-Devil: New Information about Harriet Wilson and the 'Bellmont' Family," *American Literature* 65.1 (1993): 19–52; and *Our Nig*, ed. Henry Louis Gates (New York: Random House, 1983).

39. Henry Louis Gates, ed., *The Bondwoman's Narrative* (New York: Warner Books, 2002), xxi.

40. Ibid., xviii–xix.

41. In "Hannah Crafts's Sense of an Ending," William L. Andrews presents several reasons for concluding that the author of *The Bondwoman's Narrative* was probably a black woman. See Henry Louis Gates, Jr. and Hollis Robbins, eds., *In Search of Hannah Crafts* (New York: Basic Civitas, 2004), 30–42. In "*The Bondwoman's Narrative*: Text, Paratext, Intertext and Hypertext," *Journal of American Studies* 39 (2005): 147–65, Celeste-Marie Bernier and Judie Newman marshal internal evidence from the text to argue that the author of *The Bondwoman's Narrative* was not a slave but a member of the white servant class.

42. Ann duCille, *The Coupling Convention: Sex, Text, and Tradition in Black Women's Fiction* (New York: Oxford University Press, 1993), 14.

43. William Wells Brown, *Clotel; or, The President's Daughter*, ed. M. Giulia Fabi (New York: Penguin, 2004), 44–45.

44. Among the many books that have been written on mixed-blood characters in nineteenth-century American fiction, the following offer important assessments of antebellum writing in this vein: Judith Berzon, *Neither White Nor Black: The Mulatto Character in American Fiction* (New York: New York University Press, 1978); James Kinney, *Amalgamation! Race, Sex, and Rhetoric in the Nineteenth-Century American Novel* (Westport, CT: Greenwood, 1985); Werner Sollors, *Neither Black nor White yet Both: Thematic Explorations of Interracial Literature* (New York: Oxford University Press, 1997); M. Giulia Fabi, *Passing and the Rise of the African American Novel* (Urbana: University of Illinois Press, 2001); Cassandra Jackson, *Barriers Between Us: Interracial Sex in Nineteenth-Century American Literature* (Bloomington: Indiana University Press, 2004); and Betsy Erkkila, *Mixed Bloods and Other Crosses* (Philadelphia: University of Pennsylvania Press, 2005).

45. See, for instance, Metta Victoria Victor, *Maum Guinea, and Her Plantation "Children"* (New York: Beadle, 1861), "one of the most successful dime novels ever," according to James Kinney (*Amalgamation!*, 79); H. L. Hosmer, *Adela, the Quadroon* (Columbia, OH: Follett, Foster, 1860); John T. Trowbridge, *Neighbor Jackwood* (Boston: Phillips, Sampson, 1857); Mayne Reid, *The Quadroon* (New York: Robert M. DeWitt, 1856); and E.D.E.N. Southworth, *Retribution* (New York: Harper, 1849). In all these novels mixed-race women end up in happy marriages to white lovers. Examples of antebellum fiction in which a mixed-race woman dies tragically include Lydia Maria Child, "The Quadroons," *Fact and Fiction* (New York: Frances, 1846) and Elizabeth Livermore, *Zoe, or, The Quadroon's Triumph*, 2 vols. (Cincinnati: Truman, 1855).

46. See William L. Andrews, "Miscegenation in the Late Nineteenth-Century American Novel," in *Interracialism: Black-White Intermarriage in American History, Literature, and Law*, ed. Werner Sollors (New York: Oxford University Press, 2000), 305–13.

47. Judith Berzon, *Neither White Nor Black*, 98–100; Suzanne Bost, *Mulattas and Mestizas* (Athens: University of Georgia Press, 2003), 60–61.

48. Werner Sollors, "'Never Was Born': The Mulatto, an American Tragedy?" *Massachusetts Review* 27 (1986): 293–315; Hazel Carby, *Reconstructing Womanhood: The Emergence of the Afro-American Woman Novelist* (New York: Oxford University Press, 1987), 87–94.

49.   See J. Noel Heermance, *Clotelle: A Tale of the Southern States* in *William Wells Brown and Clotelle* (North Haven, CT: Shoe String Press, Inc., 1969), 57.

50.   Veta Smith Tucker has developed a reading of *The Curse of Caste* as a commentary on the Civil War in "A Tale of Disunion: The Politics of Unclaimed Kindred in Julia C. Collins's *The Curse of Caste; or, The Slave Bride*," unpublished paper delivered at the American Studies Association Annual Meeting, Atlanta, Georgia, November 11, 2004.

51.   In the short story "Her Virginia Mammy," *The Wife of His Youth* (Boston: Houghton Mifflin, 1899), Charles W. Chesnutt portrays an African American parent's decision to withhold from her daughter the knowledge of her racial ancestry, thereby allowing her to pass unknowingly as a white woman.

Editorial Note

The principal purpose of this edition of the work of Julia C. Collins is to reprint each text as a faithful reproduction of its original. This edition does not attempt to modernize or regularize spelling, capitalization, italicization, or paragraphing in Collins's texts to conform to twenty-first-century style or practice. Obvious inconsistencies in spelling within a given text, indicative of a printer's error, have been silently corrected. Words that are spelled two different ways, such as the proper name Hartly, also spelled Hartley, in various parts of *The Curse of Caste*, are rendered throughout the text in the spelling in which they first appear in the original text. Terms such as Negro, Christian, or the Bible, which were often not capitalized in Collins's time, remain as they appeared when they were originally published in the *Christian Recorder*. In order to preserve the intention and flavor of the original text, the editors have made no wording changes, but they have minimally altered Collins's punctuation to eliminate run-on sentences; to add missing but needed punctuation, such as dropped quotation marks;

and to delete punctuation that appears to have been added for no reason, such as commas between subjects and verbs of sentences. All annotations of Collins's texts are provided by the editors.

Chapters III, XII, XVII, and XXX of *The Curse of Caste* have yet to be located. These chapters appeared respectively in the March 11, May 13, June 17, and September 16, 1865, issues of the *Christian Recorder*. Any information about where these missing issues of the *Recorder* might be located would be gratefully appreciated by the editors of this volume.

—Anne Bruder

THE CURSE OF CASTE;
OR THE SLAVE BRIDE

CHAPTER I.   February 25, 1865

"My school-days are over, and now farewell to books and quiet happiness," said Claire Neville, with a sigh, on the morning following the closing exercises of L—Seminary,[1] as she was gathering books, papers, pens, and drawing materials with sundry other articles pertaining to boarding school life, into an indiscriminate mass, preparatory to packing them away. "I am weak and foolish, I know," said Claire aloud, "to feel so badly about leaving old friends and associations, to go forth into a cold and uncharitable world, but I can not help it. As my very soul shrinks from coming in contact with strangers, who will not understand my nature, and, therefore, cannot sympathize with me." And the proud head was bowed upon her clasped hands, and bright, pearly tears were falling thick and fast. "Just one moment of weakness," murmured she, "and I shall be strong again, strong to do and dare." Claire Neville formed a beautiful and striking picture as she sat, with bowed head and drooping figure, the seeming embodiment of grief; for Claire was strangely, wildly, and darkly beautiful. Hers was that rich tropical loveliness, consisting of a tall, well-developed form, with rare, creamy complexion, cheeks like full-blown damask roses, eyes of midnight blackness, overshadowed by slightly arching brows of the same jetty hue, a broad, pure forehead, bound by a wealth of purple black hair, which in its natural loveliness enveloped her like a cloud, and a perfect mouth, disclosing rows of even, pearl-white teeth, formed, in all, a picture so strikingly beautiful, that once beheld, you voluntarily turn to gaze again. Claire was so absorbed

3

in grief that she noted not the opening of the door, nor the bright sunbeam that entered with the person of a lovely young girl, until a gentle hand rested caressingly on the drooping head, and a sweet voice murmured, in slightly surprised accents:

"Dear Claire in tears, can it be possible that you have a grief unshared by me? But tell me darling, what is it that disturbs you so?" said Ella Summers, pausing. But failing to elicit a reply, said this time, with pained expression of countenance and quivering lip, "Cannot you trust me, who have always endeavored to be a true friend?"

"Forgive me, Ella dear, if by my silence I have wounded your gentle heart, for believe me, you are the dearest friend I have on earth, and there is none to whom I would reveal my inmost heart, as I have to you. But I cannot help feeling the bitter isolation of my life."

"Let us speak of something else," said Ella, "You are despondent, I see."

Claire smiled faintly, while Ella resumed: "I have just received a long letter from mamma, in which she desires me to bring my friend Claire home with me, to make a long visit; and you will go, of course," she added, coaxingly, "and we will have a splendid time; for brother Charles is coming home to spend vacation, and cousins Harry and Fanny Leeburn are coming to spend the summer months with us, down by the lake. Such rides, such pic-nics, and sails by moonlight on the silvery lake, as will astound the simple natives of Ashton. Why, it is exhilarating, even to think of, after a season of such unremitting study as we have had."

Claire was deeply moved by her friend's disinterested kindness, and replied, in a voice tremulous with emotion, "Dear Ella, I hope you will not deem me ungrateful if I decline your much tempting invitation, as it pains me to refuse that which would afford me so much real pleasure."

"Then, why do you decline?" said Ella, her blue eyes extended a trifle beyond their usual width with astonishment, "when you acknowledge it gives you pain to refuse, and would impart pleasure to accept."

"Ella," responded Claire, with great frankness, all traces of former weakness effectually banished, "you are inexpressibly dear to me, and your past friendship will shed a gentle halo over the gloom of many hours to come in the dark, untried future, but you don't understand my position in life—how wide the differences between your lot and mine. While you are the child of wealth and position, I am the child of poverty and misfortune!"

Claire was rapidly pacing the floor now, her queenly form drawn to the proudest height. Ella had never, during their long acquaintance, seen her uniformly quiet and reserved friend in such an excited state of mind, so she wisely forbore interrupting her, and was content to look the astonishment she dared not express. Claire continued:

"You have a host of kind and loving friends to cherish and protect you, who make your pleasure a constant study, and seek to anticipate your every wish, while I am homeless and almost friendless—have never known a mother's kind, protecting care, and I don't know that I even have a right to the name I bear. I know nothing of my mother, not even her name. I know not if a shadow rested on her fair fame. The only link between my past and present life, is an old beloved nurse, named Juno,[2] whom, I am confident, knows all, but I can prevail upon her to impart nothing. I am even indebted to a person unknown for my education, except that I saw him several times during my earlier years. It is six years now since I saw him. So you can not fail to see the disparity of our social positions, and, therefore, must acknowledge how utterly impossible it is for us to retain our old relation, now that our school days are over; nor would your mother desire it, if she knew all, and I should sacrifice my self respect; if I intruded myself upon her friendship and hospitality in any other than my true position."

Ella now ventured to remonstrate, "O Claire, you mustn't think what you have just told can make the least difference in my feelings toward you, for I love you now better than ever, and I know my dear mamma too well to think that she would love you less, because you fail to know who your parents were. It is one phase of life we fail to read, and to know you, Claire, is only to know that your parents, whatever obscurity rests on them, were persons of purity and refinement."

Claire looked up gratefully, and said, "I feel, too, my parents were pure and good; it is only when I think of the vague mystery that surrounds my birth and parentage, that the doubt comes."

"Claire dear, believe my words prophetic when I say the time will come when all will be made clear, and you will find in your parents all your loving heart could wish. Cannot you trust me?"

"Yes, Ella, I can and do trust you, but with the trust comes the presentiment of sorrow connected with the revelation. But I will cease to repine, and will school myself to hope that all will yet be well."

After conversing some time longer, Ella found that Claire was firm in declining to make the proposed visit. She asked Claire what she intended doing, now that their school-days were over.

CHAPTER II.   March 4, 1865

"I shall try the life of a governess," said Claire, quietly smiling at the dissatisfaction mirrored in her friend's expressive countenance.

"But," said Ella, "you will necessarily have to wait some time ere you can obtain a position that would be desirable."

"Not so," said Claire. "I have a situation already, and have only to make preparations to take my respective position in life."

"Now, Claire!" exclaimed Ella, with lively interest, "tell me all about it."

"There is but little to tell," said Claire, "but that little you shall know. Our dear preceptress, Miss Ellwood, received a letter from an old school friend, who married, years ago, Col. Tracy, a rich Southern gentleman, and went to reside in New Orleans. But some trouble in their family, relative to the marriage of a son, has rendered Mrs. Tracy, for years, a confirmed invalid. Seeing one of the circulars of L— Seminary, she observed the name of Miss Maria Ellwood as preceptress; and, knowing it could be none other than the Maria of school-day remembrances, she wrote her a long and interesting letter, which proved the correctness of her supposition. She also requested Miss Ellwood to get a young lady of suitable qualifications, to be a companion for her, and act as governess to two little girls, aged respectively ten and twelve years, offering an excellent salary; and Miss Ellwood, knowing my intention of becoming a governess, offered me the situation, saying, 'She knew of no one she would so cheerfully recommend.' So I have accepted the situation, and shall start South with a Mr. and Mrs. Harrington, friends of Mrs. Tracy who have been North, and have kindly consented to take me under their charge. So you see my path is marked out, and I have only time to follow it."

"Well, Claire Neville, I think you have taken sudden leave of your senses, going South to be a governess and companion to an invalid and two little girls. 'Hypochondrian' and 'hoydens,'[1] which words, I suppose, would be well substituted for invalid and little girls. I can well imagine what your life would be," exclaimed Ella, vehemently. "And should there be a young man in the question,—"

"There is one in the family," interrupted Claire, merrily.

"As there has been trouble about one son's marriage," replied Ella, "they will be in perpetual fear of the beautiful Yankee governess, and you will be kept back on all and every occasion."

"I think," said Claire, a little haughtily, "I shall know my place so well, that the snubbing, as you term it, will be quite unnecessary."

"And," continued Ella, "if there is a grown daughter, and should she, by chance, be handsome, she will be jealous of you. I can tell you, Claire, I would never be governess in a Southern family."

Claire replied, by saying: "Miss Belle Tracy is very beautiful, and is considered the belle of New Orleans."

"It matters not," said Ella, "if you will go, I sincerely hope you may be happy in your new position."

"I leave at one o'clock," said Claire, looking at her watch, "so I must go and make my adieus."

"But, Claire," said Ella, "in your new life do not forget your Ella."

A few more parting words, a few tears, a loving embrace, and the friends parted.

Claire, indeed, knew nothing of her past life. She never knew a mother's care. Juno, an old colored nurse, had taken care of her as long as she could remember. No friends had ever visited them, with the exception of a tall, dark man, who came at long intervals, and always had long talks with Juno concerning Claire. He often tried to win the confidence of the dark beautiful child, but to no purpose; for Claire shrank from him with instinctive dislike. They lived thus together, Juno and the lovely little girl, until Claire had reached her twelfth year, when, closely following the last visit of the handsome but repulsive stranger, Claire was placed at the L— Seminary, where she remained for six years, happy in the love of her schoolmates and kind preceptress, Miss Ellwood.

At the last mentioned visit of the stranger, Claire remembered to have heard him frequently repeat the name of Richard. Who was Richard she wondered? And she instinctively felt that he was, in some way or other, connected with her past life. On entering the room after the stranger had gone, she observed a handkerchief lying on the floor. She picked it up to examine it, and found in one corner the name of George Manville. Claire said nothing to Juno, but resolved to retain the handkerchief, asking herself many times— "Who is George Manville?"

Claire was not long in preparing her simple wardrobe, and went to pay Juno a visit, who was delighted to see her dear child, but loud in her remonstrances against Claire's going South; but when Claire mentioned the name of Colonel Tracy, her excitement was without bounds, as she exclaimed: "Miss Claire, for the love of heaven, don't go to be governess in the old Colonel's family. What would Master Richard say to your going to be governess in the Tracy family?"

"Who and what is Richard? And what is he to me?" interrupted Claire, in an eager tone.

Juno felt that she had committed herself, and, therefore, could not be induced to say another word about Richard, whoever he might be, but continued to entreat Claire to forego going South. But Claire was firm in her resolution to go. Juno, finding it quite useless to remonstrate, resigned herself to listen to Claire's plans, which, when ended, she said, with clouded brow and sad voice, "Dear child, I fear you will see great sorrow, and will often wish you had taken poor old Juno's advice, and never gone to be a governess in that proud family. Yes, poor child," she continued, "I know your poor heart will feel many a hard pang, but I will never cease to pray for you, darling, and," she added, doubtfully, "I hope you may be happy."

Claire felt Juno's words to be an echo of her own feelings.

"I have something to give you," said Juno, leaving the room. She quickly returned, however, bringing with her a little rosewood box, from which she lifted a beautiful ring of strange and exquisite workmanship. She handed it to Claire, simply saying, "It was your mother's."

Claire gazed on the glittering circlet with tearful eyes. On an inner plate were the initials *R.T. to L.* Claire examined it a long while, then placed it on her own slender finger. The parting, between the faithful old nurse and the child she had watched over so long, was touching in the extreme.

Now that we have introduced Juno to our readers, she will appear, from time to time, with the other characters who play an important part in the following narrative.

CHAPTER IV.   March 18, 1865

This was not a difficult matter, as the Count was pleased at first sight with Isabelle, who was, indeed, the most fascinating woman he had ever met. Thus things were progressing in the Tracy family when Claire entered it as governess. Count Sayvord was unremitting in attention to Isabelle, and she inordinately jealous if he deviated in the slightest. But, thus far, the Count had failed in reading her true character.

But, to do the young man justice, we will add that he had thought but little of marriage—but little as connected with Isabelle Tracy. There was a nameless something which always deterred him from broaching the subject, when frequent opportunities occurred; and Isabelle secretly wondered why he did not propose.

Col. Tracy was proud of Isabelle's great beauty, and he secretly hoped she might win young Sayvord, whom he had reason to consider a desirable match for his favorite child.

After tea, Claire retired with Laura and Nellie while the others adjourned to the parlors. Claire spent another hour with Mrs. Tracy, and then retired to the room assigned her, which was light, airy and pleasant; and, when she was at liberty to indulge in her own reflections, she felt pleased with her situation, and thought she should like it; but, when she thought of Isabelle Tracy's searching black eyes, a cold chill ran through her, for there was something so repelling in that cold, haughty glance, which seemed to scintillate hatred. She tried to forget it, but turn which way she would those great black eyes were before her! Did it augur evil, or what? Her dreams were an odd mixture of "black eyes and blue."[1]

The morning dawned beautifully, and Claire walked out on the verandah to inhale the morning air. As she came forth, she was met by Laura and Nellie, who were anxiously awaiting her appearance, and, each taking a hand, led her forth chatting the while in a lively strain. Roses, cape-jessamines, and crape myrtle were in profusion, and Claire being a passionate lover of flowers, was delighted with the beauty and luxuriance of the floral shrubbery. At almost every step she encountered the curious gaze of the negroes, who looked wonderingly at her.

After following various paths and windings, they came suddenly upon a beautiful arbor almost embowered in orange trees.

Claire was about to express her delight when she observed, extended at full length, reading, the young Count Sayvord, who arose at their entrance, bowed politely, and would have withdrawn, but that they passed on without stopping and continued their rambles until the bell summoned them to breakfast. As they came up to the house, Isabelle was standing on the verandah and bowed coldly, and again Claire shuddered as she encountered the piercing glance which seemed to read her very soul. They passed on to the breakfast room, and were soon followed by the Count and Isabelle, who was covered with smiles and blushes. Claire noticed and wondered at the change.

After breakfast, Claire repaired to Mrs. Tracy's room, ready to begin her new duties. Mrs. Tracy thought, as it was now Thursday, they would not commence any lessons until the following Monday, and that Claire was at liberty to use her time as she pleased, much of which she spent in the company of the invalid, who was mild and affectionate, quite unlike her proud daughter.

On Friday evening, after tea, as they were leaving the tea-room, Laura said, "Oh, Miss Neville, you have not sung for us, yet."

"Yes," chimed in little Nellie, "you promised you would."

"I hope Miss Neville will not refuse," said Lloyd Tracy, with an encouraging smile, while Sayvord's look expressed the interest he felt in her answer.

Col. Tracy, at this moment, came forward, and placing Claire's little hand within his arm, led the way to the parlor, saying, "They would not take a refusal." So Claire consented, notwithstanding the haughty displeasure expressed in Isabelle's countenance.

Claire took her seat at the piano with quiet dignity and the utmost composure, which only seemed to annoy Miss Tracy, who hoped at least to detect some frustration of manner, but in vain, for Claire, after playing a short prelude, glided into a beautiful song, and, as her rich clear voice swelled on the air, every voice save the singer's was hushed.

Lloyd arose, as if impelled by some unseen power, and came to Claire's side; Col. Tracy was strangely affected, and was walking the floor with perturbed mien;[2] and Sayvord never once withdrew his gaze from the face of the songstress. Isabelle, alone, seemed unmoved.

After the song was ended, Sayvord requested another, and the little girls and Lloyd warmly seconded the request. Claire, with Lloyd's assistance, sang several songs of great beauty and pathos.

Claire possessed a voice of unusual depth and sweetness, and Miss Ellwood early noticing her great talent for music, both vocal and instrumental, had afforded her every possible advantage for improvement, and the result was her musical powers were highly cultivated.

After the songs were ended, Claire bade them a courteous "good evening," and retired in company with Laura and Nellie.

A long silence ensued, broken only by Col. Tracy's steady tread when he abruptly turned to Lloyd, saying in a husky tone, "Is there any one of whom Miss Neville reminds you?"

Lloyd started perceptibly, and briefly answered, "Richard."

Sayvord and Isabelle had walked to the window opening on the verandah, and were just passing out when the name of Miss Neville arrested the attention of Sayvord, whose thoughts were still with the singer. He noticed the question asked with an anxiety of manner and eagerness of tone, as though he hoped, yet feared the reply, and Lloyd's brief answer, "Richard," caused the Count to give a low whistle of surprise, quite forgetting the lady at his side, who was thoughtfully tearing to pieces a beautiful rose and scattering the leaves at her feet. She had heard neither the question nor the answer.

Sayvord now knew why it was that Claire's face always seemed familiar, and why her voice always arrested his attention by its very sadness; it was the striking resemblance she bore to an American gentleman he had met at his uncle Clayburch Sayvord's country seat, in France, whose sad voice and melancholy face had haunted him for a long time. What could it all mean? Was Claire indeed a relative of that strange, dark man, over whom a shadow seemed to have fallen, and, if so, why should she occupy the position she did in Col. Tracy's house? Sayvord was sorely at his wit's end; but he determined to fathom the mystery that enveloped the young governess. He dismissed the subject from his thoughts, for the present, and began a lively conversation with Isabelle.

Col. Tracy sat in his arm chair buried in thought, and, seemingly, not of the most pleasant nature. Lloyd was extended at full length on one of the garden sofas, quietly enjoying a segar and looking at the moon, but it was quite evident that his thoughts were otherwise engaged, for, ever and anon, he murmured, "Poor Dick, I cannot but pity, while I blame him. It was a sad blow for one so young and gifted as he. And the beautiful but ill-fated Lina! How he must have loved her to encounter the rage of my proud, passionate father who would rather have slain him with his own hand than have had the disgrace of that marriage. Poor Dick!" he concluded with a deep sigh.

A spirit of disquietude seemed to have taken possession of all. Claire, when she bade the children good night and paid a last visit to the invalid, sought her own room; the moon shone brightly on the floor, and flooded the room with a soft light. Claire, drawing her chair to the open window, fell into a deep reverie. Her thoughts naturally reverted to her northern home. She thought of Miss Ellwood, of all her kindness through her lonely childhood, of Juno's last words, and her own presentiment of evil; a feeling of sadness pervaded her soul as memory lingered over the scenes of the past. She looked at Juno's parting gift through tear-dimmed eyes; the little circlet glittered in the moonlight as the bright tear-drops fell on its shining surface. Why could not Juno have told her just a little of the mother she had never known? What dark mystery surrounded her father? She would rather know the worst than always live in suspense, dreading something she knew not what. Why was she not born happy and careless, like Rosa, the nimble-fingered, light-footed creature, who was always smiling, and never seemed to have a thought beyond pleasing her mistress and the children, whom she fairly worshipped?

Claire was thoroughly unhappy, and she at last retired to rest. But, it seemed, sleep had fled her pillow; for a long while she tossed restlessly about, sometimes thinking of Isabelle's cold manner and fierce black eyes; then of Sayvord's earnest gaze, and Lloyd's respectful attention; then she wondered at the likeness she bore to the Tracy's. It was singular, to say the least, and she felt herself an object of curiosity even to the negroes, who regarded her wonderingly, and talked mysteriously of somebody and something Claire knew not what. At last sleep came to her relief, and happiness dawned on her troubled mind.

CHAPTER V.   March 25, 1865

A Heart's History.

Col. Tracy's father, or old John Tracy, as he was familiarly designated, was a Connecticut man, but had emigrated to Louisiana, bought himself a plantation well stocked with slaves (that indispensable appendage of southern life) worked it, multiplied the negroes, and at last died immensely rich, leaving his vast property to be equally divided between Col. Tracy, who was then a young man of twenty-one years of age, and his sister Laura, a young lady of seventeen years, who were the only living heirs of John Tracy, whose young wife had died in giving birth to the infant Laura years ago, in their New England home.

Laura had always resided in the North with an old maiden aunt, who, unlike most old maids we read of, was as gentle, cheerful, and dark-eyed a little woman as you could wish to see. She was greatly attached to her young niece, and Laura had never felt the loss of the mother her infant eyes had never beheld.

The winter previous to John Tracy's death, his fast failing health caused him often to think of the home of his youth, and at last, to write a letter to his only sister, inviting her to come and make his house her home, because he longed for the faces of his own kin-dred and was wearied of the dusky countenances of the negroes, who were flitting in and out of their humble efforts to aid the lonely, and, not infrequently, irritable master.

Miss Tracy, on being apprised of her brother's illness, accompa-nied by Laura, went south, and, by their united efforts, succeeded in cheering the lone invalid and rendering his last moments happy, by kind attention and loving care.

One lovely afternoon, just as the sun was sinking behind a bank of crimson clouds, John Tracy had all the slaves brought, one by one, to his bed-side, and took an affectionate leave of all; and, when the daylight was fast fading into darkness, surrounded by a group of weeping negroes, his head supported on the bosom of his lov-ing sister, Frank and Laura kneeling, grief-stricken, at his bed-side, the soul of John Tracy passed from earth away–passed from death unto life.

After the remains of John Tracy were consigned to their last rest-ing place, and all other matters relating to the effects of the de-ceased parent properly adjusted, the old house, which was always lonely, but now more desolate than ever, was locked up, the plantation and negroes left to the care of a trusty overseer, Miss Tracy, with Laura and Frank, started for her northern home.

Laura was delighted to see her old home again, and hovered like a bird over each familiar object, while Frank only shrugged his shoulders, saying that the North was too bleak and cold for him, and that he should soon seek his sunny, southern home, where roses bloomed the year round.

"But man proposes, and God disposes."[1] Frank was destined to fall hopelessly and irretrievably in love with brown-eyed, brown-haired Nellie Thornton, a sweet and winsome little maiden who was Laura's dearest friend.

Thus, the Winter wore away. Spring came with its burden of flowers, sunshine and showers. Summer waned into Autumn. Still Frank lingered in the little New England village; and, when he did start for his home, it was but to return again to bear to his southern home a beautiful northern bride.

Thus, Nellie Thornton became the wife of him we shall know hereafter as Col. Tracy, and went to preside over the heart and home of him to whom she had given herself and trusted with her heart's first love. A year was wafted by on the wings of time, when a beautiful boy came to bless their happy union; and for years little Richard's was the only voice that rung in childish glee, and his the only little feet that pattered through the great halls. Then came little Lillie, who lived but one short year, and then a little, short grave in the old cemetery marked the last resting place of the flower that was too fair and fragile for earth. Then came a pair of twins, beautiful, cherubic boys, who smiled on earth but a few short months when the fell destroyer came again, and little Frank and Willie were laid, side by side, in their white-robed beauty, in their cold, silent tombs.

Gentle Nellie Tracy grieved long and deeply over her lost treasures, and little Richard became again their only and idolized child. For some years none other came to bless.

At the age of sixteen, Richard was sent to college. A year later, an event occurred which shed joy over the silent household. Little Lloyd Tracy came to brighten the gloom of the old homestead; and, in the course of years other children were added, whom we will have occasion to introduce hereafter; but, for awhile we leave them to their quiet happiness, while we follow the fortune of young Richard.

Richard, after passing a successful collegiate course and graduating with honor, was on his return home, down the noble Mississippi on board the beautiful steamer Alhambra,[2] when he formed the acquaintance of a party of fellow-travelers, one of whom deeply interested him. The party consisted of two young ladies and a gentleman, who registered their names as Hartly. The gentleman was the brother of one of the ladies, while the other lady seemed only a distant relative.

The brother and sister, whom we shall call Ralph and Mary, appeared to be much absorbed with some topic, the nature of which apparently greatly annoyed them. There was something distant and repelling in their treatment of the second young lady, whom we will call *Lina*. Richard was interested in the young stranger from his first acquaintance, and her apparent loneliness enlisted his warmest sympathies. Thus he came to spend much of his time, which would otherwise have passed drearily enough, in her society.

Lina was as beautiful as the fancied image of a poet's dream: a form of medium size, with dark flashing eyes and a profusion of curling black hair, which defied all efforts on her part to keep in bands or braids, but would, naturally, fall in graceful ringlets about her neck and shoulders. One singular feature in Lina's beauty was her dark, rich-looking complexion; she was not a brunette, but hers was that dark brownish skin which we observe in the Spaniard and half-breed Indians, which, combined with features of striking regularity, rendered Lina, as she indeed was, a singularly attractive young lady.

Lina possessed a voice of sweet and thrilling power, and Richard never wearied of hearing her sing those old ballads, which she sang with such deep pathos and exquisite feeling. She soon learned to watch for his coming, and blushed beautifully when he bent to whisper some impassioned strain, or allowed his dark eloquent eyes to rest earnestly on her down-cast face. They sought not to analyze their feelings; they were happy, and that was enough.

But the trip down the Mississippi, like all earthly things, must have an end. On the last night of their voyage, the moon shone clear and bright as Richard and Lina were walking the deck of the Alhambra, her hand resting on his arm. It seemed, indeed, a fitting time to disclose their tale of love; and, from Lina's blushing, down-cast face and Richard's proud and happy bearing, it was quite evident that his had been a successful wooing. Lina was the first to speak:

"Richard," she said, while something like sadness vibrated through her voice, "I fear my happiness is too great to last. A presentiment of evil hovers over me. It is foolish, no doubt," she added, as Richard began smiling, "but I cannot divine why Ralph and Mary treat me so strangely. I always believed we were sisters, notwithstanding the difference in our appearance and dispositions. Mary is my senior by two years. Our father placed us in the convent as sisters to be educated, and we have there remained, being frequently visited by our father, who was always good and kind. But since Ralph Hartly came for us, there has been a marked change in the deportment of Mary, while Ralph, I verily believe, hates me; for I often look up and find him gazing at me with an expression that is almost fiendish. I may be penniless or even worse. I know not what this conduct presages. And Richard," the little hand pressing his arm more firmly, "perhaps you would cease to love me, and, if so, I should die." This was said in a low, firm voice, entirely free from passion.

Richard needed but one glance in the dark, truthful eyes of Lina to be assured of her earnestness, when he replied with deep emotion: "Lina, whatever be your fate or fortune, I will never desert you, so help me God! I will make you my own dear wife; my arm shall protect you, and all the love of my warm, true heart shall be yours. Lina, do I look like one who would speak lightly or break a vow once made? No power on earth shall take you from me!"

Lina silently placed her hand in Richard's, saying, "I trust you; I cannot doubt you now."

So absorbed was each in the conversation of the other, that they had not noticed the change in the heavens. Piles of black clouds were rising in the West, and had almost obscured the fair face of the moon, when a loud peel of thunder startled them, and, for the first time, they noticed that all the other passengers had retired to the cabins and state-rooms, and they were about following their example, when a vivid flash of lightning and a few large drops of rain hurried their exit from the deck. At the door of the ladies' cabin, Richard bade Lina good night.

The storm raged for an hour, and then cleared away, the moon shining brightly as ever. Many of the gentlemen returned on deck, among whom were Richard and Ralph Hartly. Richard had often conversed with Ralph and always found him courteous and gentlemanly in deportment; but there was a nameless something about him which alternately attracted and repelled him. On this occasion, the gentlemen merely exchanged a few common place remarks, as each appeared to be buried in his own reflections.

On the following morning, as the Alhambra neared the beautiful Crescent City, Richard sought Lina aside to exchange a few last words. Lina told him they were going to Hartly Hall, on her father's plantation, about fifty miles above New Orleans. So Richard parted with Lina, promising to visit her father soon, which recalled one of Lina's blushes, and a bright crystal drop fell on the hand that clasped her own; a moment more, and they were lost to view in the hurrying crowd. Theirs was indeed a bright dream! Would it ever be realized?

CHAPTER VI. April 1, 1865

Richard was warmly greeted by his parents, and the negroes were jubilant over massa's return. Mrs. Tracy felt proud of the great, tall, noble-looking youth, who stooped to kiss her still blooming cheek. And well might she feel proud, for never was a nobler, better son given to gladden a mother's heart.

Col. Tracy took especial pride in introducing his son to all his acquaintances, but was horrified and dismayed to hear Richard give expression to many anti-slavery principles, which he had imbibed while at the North. He tried to reason with him about the absurdity of entertaining such notions as social equality between races so widely divergent, in every respect, as the white and black. But Richard stoutly adhered to his belief that it was wrong for one man to enslave another, and keep in bondage a human being, having a mind and soul susceptible of improvement and cultivation.

Col. Tracy found too much of his own spirit infused into his son's character to think of eradicating these sentiments by argument, but trusted to time and the influence of southern principles and society to effect the desired change. Thus the subject was dropped, and both father and son avoided alluding to it again.

Richard, while at a party made in honor of his return, formed the acquaintance of a young man by the name of George Manville. Young Manville was a gay, good-looking fellow, good-natured and perfectly well acquainted with the city and the circle in which Richard moved. They soon became fast friends. Manville was rich and handsome, and much sought after by those who failed in reading his true character, as did Richard Tracy. But Manville was a villain—the beautiful casket enshrined a heart black as the shadows of Hades,[1] and dead to all the finer feelings, those minor chords which render the life of man replete with living beauty.

Richard sometimes felt the subtle influence that this Manville exerted over him without understanding it; however, for candid and honorable himself, he did not readily doubt others. These two men were fated to be connected in a degree through life.

One morning, at breakfast, Col. Tracy declared his intention of going up to the plantation for a few days on business. We will here state that Col. Tracy had moved to the city of New Orleans, the old homestead being occupied by his overseer's family.

During his father's absence, Richard usually spent the mornings with his mother and little Lloyd. He told her of his love for the beautiful Lina, of their betrothal, and her singular presentiment of evil. Mrs. Tracy was interested in the unknown girl, whose cause her son pleaded so eloquently.

"You would only need see her, to love her," he said, persuasively.

Mrs. Tracy did not doubt that Lina was all Richard's fond imagination painted, but she asked:

"Do you know any thing of this family of Hartlys? You know your father's prejudice against persons marrying with those beneath them in rank and fortune, no matter what their qualities may be."

"I know, mother," said the young man, "but should Lina become poor by any untoward circumstance, that is no reason why I should seek to absolve the vows registered in the sight of Heaven. Of Lina's family I know nothing. I only know she is good and pure.

I hope, for my father's sake, she may be rich and her family such as he would desire my alliance with. But, my gentle mother, whatever misfortune may befall Lina, I will marry her just the same."

"God bless you, my noble son," said Nellie Tracy, with deep feeling. "I trust all may be well."

That same morning Richard's portrait was sent home. It had been painted by a celebrated artist, who had succeeded admirably in giving the picture a true and life-like expression. Before they had finished hanging the picture, Manville was announced, and with the freedom of a privileged friend, came into the room. When at last the picture was hung in a proper position, with just enough light to give a good effect, all stood back to take a full view of it. Mrs. Tracy remembered, years after, the feelings she experienced when that picture was hung. All were pleased and expressed their satisfaction.

When Col. Tracy returned from his visit to the plantation, he told Richard, in the presence of Manville and Mrs. Tracy, that he had made a very foolish investment. All looked inquiringly at him.

"I attended a sale of slaves, the property of old Hartly, who resides about fifty miles up the river, and was formerly a man of considerable wealth, but being of a wild, reckless disposition, has, in a few years, squandered his fortune, and degenerated into a confirmed drunkard and gambler. I purchased several plantation and house servants among whom is a beautiful quadroon[2], who is the daughter of old Hartly, I understand, and has been educated at a Catholic school, in Canada, and believed herself his lawful child. The young girl is beautiful, and I think, well educated. Her distress was really affecting, and, out of pity for the young thing, I bought her with the lot, but what I am to do with the baggage,[3] I cannot conceive, for slaves educated at the North are not just the thing to be introduced into a southern household. So, I guess I will sell this bit of humanity at the first offer. Why she had the audacity to faint, when, by accident, she learned the name of her future master was Col. Tracy. I must say, although I claim to be a kind and indulgent master, I have no use for this sensitive class of negroes."

Col. Tracy, at this juncture, noticed the effect of his language upon his wife and son, which seemed to him as singular as it was inexplicable. Mrs. Tracy looked pale and horrified, while Richard's pale and almost defiant expression betokened a fixed resolution, although he uttered not a word, and soon left the house, accompanied by Manville. Mrs. Tracy soon left the room also, and Col. Tracy was the sole occupant, and was at liberty to digest his astonishment as best he might.

A few hours later, Manville returned, and after a long conference with Col. Tracy, departed with the document in his pocket, which pronounced him lawful owner of the young quadroon.

Richard returned at tea time with seeming composure, but his mother's eye penetrated the veil. She alone read his feelings, and felt the resolution he had taken. Her heart was too full for utterance, when, after tea, Richard motioned her to follow him. He led the way to the library. A long time elapsed ere they appeared again. Mrs. Tracy was deeply agitated, while Richard's face still wore the same determined expression. What passed during that strange conference, none ever knew. Richard followed his mother to the parlor, when he kissed her gently, saying fervently:

"Mother, pray for me. I hope all may yet be well. Pray for Lina, too. Poor child! God knows she needs your prayers."

A moment more, and Mrs. Tracy was alone. Richard had gone. Where this would all end, she could not tell.

One beautiful morning, in a quiet New England village, far from their own home, Richard Tracy and the beautiful quadroon, Lina, were united for life. It was a quiet bridal, witnessed only by

Manville and Richard's aunt, whom we have known as Col. Tracy's sister Laura, while Laura's husband performed the rite, which united this ill-fated couple.

We will here state that all correspondence had ceased, long years ago, between Laura Tracy and her brother. Her marriage with a poor minister, Alfred Hays, had incurred his lasting displeasure. Laura had several times sought to conciliate her brother, but without success. Alfred Hays was good and noble, and with his lovely wife, joined his efforts to make the young bride happy.

Richard was happy, and soon the shadows left Lina's fair brow. They were happy, but it was as the calm that precedes the raging storm. Did Richard—did Lina—feel its dread coming? Had they no warning of the shadow, that would soon fall, crushing the life from their young hearts?

CHAPTER VII.   April 8, 1865

Lina's Home.

Richard and Lina were indeed truly happy. Little they thought of the future that loomed so darkly before them. They were happy in each other's love, and therefore content. Alfred Hays and his gentle wife smiled serenely upon the young pair, but wondered how this strange affair would end.

Manville remained until he could not help but feel that he was *de trop*,[1] when he reluctantly took his departure for the South. Richard entrusted him with an important letter to his father, which letter Manville promised faithfully to deliver into the hands of Col. Tracy immediately upon his arrival in New Orleans.

Soon after Richard's marriage, Alfred Hays received an appointment in a thriving Western village, to which he cheerfully assented, and their beautiful home was soon to become the abode of strangers. Laura's heart clung fondly to the home in which she had passed the first years of her married life. The sale of "Rose Cottage," as Laura had fancifully named it, was often the interesting subject of discussion in the family circle. At last a happy thought dawned on Richard's mind. He proposed to purchase the little homestead.

"I think it would just answer our purpose," he said, looking inquiringly at Lina, whose eloquent eyes fully expressed her delight and satisfaction.

So Rose Cottage became the property of Richard and the home of Lina. Then followed a short season of busy preparation, and the Hays were *en route* for the far West. Rose Cottage was well named, for it was really embowered in roses and trailing vines. Roses bloomed 'neath the windows, and climbing roses blossomed o'er the door. The air was ever laden with their fragrance. Other beautiful shrubs and flowers there were, but the "sweet brier" predominated. The cottage was repainted and furnished anew, and the services of Juno, a competent colored woman who had lived with the Hays many years, were secured, and the house-keeping began. Juno was an efficient hand, and under her supervision every thing underwent an entire change, while every where Lina's exquisite taste was visible, in the arrangement of the light and elegant furniture. Curtains of a light, airy fabric were gracefully looped back from the windows, while choice paintings and exquisite engravings adorned the walls, and last, but not least in order, was a cottage piano, which was a prominent feature in the arrangement of the little parlor. And oft when the twilight was falling, and Juno was quietly knitting 'neath the shade of the lofty tamarack trees,[2] could the mingled voices of Richard and Lina be heard, freighting the fragrant air with melody. And it often happened that they prolonged their singing far into the evening, and passers would linger at the little white gate, as song after song thrilled and trembled on the night air, and long for a glimpse of the beautiful songstress, whom those more fortunate had reported as wondrously fair.

Would that this dream of happiness could last. Would that it were in my power to paint a picture with naught but scenes of beauty, but alas, no. Richard had put off the evil hour as long as possible, but now it could be averted no longer. He must return home to meet an angry father, perhaps to be disfranchised forever from that father's love.

Sad as was that too probable result, yet he did not regret the choice he had made. The half year of married life had only seemed to render Lina more dear than ever. No, he did not regret the sacrifice he had made for her sake. His father would disinherit him without doubt. But he still possessed quite a fortune in his own right, left him by a will of his great aunt, John Tracy's sister. But a father's curse is an awful thing, and that thought embittered many hours of his daily life. Yet he breathed not his fears in his young wife's ears, but always spoke hopefully of the future, though his own heart sadly misgave him, as week after week passed, and yet no answer came to the letter sent with Manville. The thought of that troubled him. He could not but fear the worst, yet he sought to keep all from Lina.

But the watchful eyes of love soon detected the change. His voice was less cheerful, his step less buoyant, and his smile less frequent. And when he did smile it was sometimes so sadly, as to bring tears to Lina's eyes. From that time she ceased to be perfectly happy. Her spirits varied with her husband's. If Richard was lively and gay, Lina was happy too, but if Richard's brow was thoughtful, or wore a look of care, the smiles faded from her lips and the rose from her cheek. Hers was a nature that could bloom while surrounded by the sunshine of love and happiness. But let them be withdrawn, let the chill breath of sorrow and adversity fall on her young heart, and the beautiful flower would droop and die.

At last Richard summoned up courage to broach the subject to his young and sensitive wife. He dreaded the effect it might have upon her excitable nature. He spoke hopefully of the result of his intended visit, for he had already noted her pale cheek and languid step. She looked frightened when he told her he was going, but she uttered not one word of remonstrance, for she felt it was his duty to go. And yet she felt that she would almost rather die than have him do so. She felt as if a cloud had suddenly enveloped his spirit. Why she dreaded to have her husband go to New Orleans, she could not tell. She would as soon have doubted the veracity of a Heavenly messenger, as to have doubted Richard's truth and fidelity.

But it was finally settled that he would start south on the following Monday, and all necessary preparations were made for his journey. He would write from every point on the route. Juno must regularly attend the village post-office, every day after the stage came in, to bring the letters, which would be anxiously waited for by the lonely little wife.

On the eventful Monday morning, when Richard was to take his departure, he gave Lina a thousand loving injunctions, as to being cheerful, taking care of her health, and so on, and playfully importuned Juno to bring the rose to his lady love's cheek ere his return. He kissed Lina "good-by," and went smiling down the walk to meet the Ruthford stage as it passed. He left her smiling and waving his handkerchief as a last adieu. Lina sought to console herself, and wait with patience for the promised letters.

CHAPTER VIII.   April 15, 1865

The Flower Fadeth.[1]

Time passed slowly with the inmates of Rose Cottage, until the
first letter would be received from Richard. Lina wandered about
the cottage and garden with a listless air, and Juno seemed more
quiet and thoughtful. She knew more of the real state of affairs
than the young wife supposed. Juno had lived so long with Laura
Hays that she was well acquainted with the history of the Tracys.
She also knew much of the character and disposition of Colonel
Frank Tracy; she was about twelve years old when Frank was married to pretty Nellie Thornton. She was then living with Laura's
aunt. Juno saw Frank Tracy once after that; it was when he came to
forbid Laura's marriage with the young minister, Alfred Hays. She
knew well his overweening family pride and love of wealth and
position. Alfred Hays was one of nature's noblemen,[2] but wealth
and position he had not. Juno was not likely to forget the terrible
family quarrel that ensued when Laura, who possessed much of
her brother's spirit and resolution, persisted in marrying the poor
minister, declaring that she had the right and was capable of choosing her own husband, and was prepared to follow the dictates of
her own heart. Frank, finding that Laura would not be persuaded
to give Alfred up, said, angrily:

"Laura, if you persist in marrying that beggar, that mere fortune hunter, you are no longer a sister of mine, so reflect well ere
you decide. I will never receive him as a brother."

He was about leaving the room when his sister's voice arrested
him. She said, in a low firm tone, "I need not time for reflection,
my decision is already made; I will marry Alfred. If he is poor, he is

good and noble, while your interference is unnatural and cruelly unjust, and—"

"Enough," cried Frank, impatiently interrupting and pushing her from him. "I will say no more; you have taken your own course, and must abide by the consequences." And he strode from the room, leaving his sister heart-stricken and aghast.

Poor Laura had not quite expected this unhappy turn affairs had taken, yet she was not prepared to sacrifice her life's happiness to her brother's selfish demands.

Frank sought his aunt, and told her the result of his interview with his sister. Laura need not indulge the hope that he would relent his cruel decision; it was unalterable. He departed without seeing Laura again, and from that time all communication between them ceased.

Not until after their marriage did Alfred Hays learn the bitter sacrifice his gentle wife had made when she fulfilled her plighted troth with him. Miss Tracy then went to reside with her niece, taking Juno with her. A few years later she died, leaving her entire fortune, with the exception of a legacy of ten thousand dollars, to her niece, Laura. The above legacy was willed to Frank Tracy's little son, Richard, to be placed in the care of Alfred Hays, until the young heir should become of age, the interest of which was payable on or after his nineteenth birthday. What had induced Miss Tracy to leave this legacy to little Richard, whom she had never seen, would be impossible to say, but future events proved the wisdom of her last act of kindness.

Juno knew all this; she also knew that all was not satisfactory in relation to Richard's marriage. She knew that some trouble was expected, though the exact nature of it she did not know, but her suspicions were very nearly correct.

Juno always had her "suspicions," and the remarkable part of it is, they were nearly always right. At last a letter came from

Richard—a kind and hopeful letter—which did much towards reviving Lina's spirits. It was soon followed by others, all written in the same hopeful, happy style, from various points on the route, and, finally, one written immediately upon his arrival in New Orleans. "Manville," he said, "was at present out of the city. I shall go home this evening. You need not look for a letter again for some time, as I shall not write until I know the final result of my visit."

Several weeks elapsed and yet no other letter came. In vain it was that Juno went to the village post-office every day, after the Ruthford stage came in; she failed to bring the white-winged messenger that would have won back the lost smile to Lina's sad face. Truly "hope deferred maketh the heart sick,"[3] for Lina's face grew more pale and sad and her step more languid, as week after week sped by, and she received no tidings from the absent one.

Every day, when it drew near the time for Juno's return from the village, she would walk down to the little gate, and wait anxiously for her coming, with eager and expectant face, but when Juno reported her ill success, she would turn away with such a look of keen disappointment, such hopeless despair as to make Juno shed tears of sympathy with the fragile creature that leaned heavily upon her arm.

At last Lina ceased to look for a letter. She never complained, but that quiet despairing look was pitiful to behold. It was in vain Juno taxed her brain in the manufacture of choice delicacies to tempt the palate of the gentle invalid, who invariably thanked her faithful friend with a sweet smile, but failed to do justice to the dainties she prepared. The golden autumn days had passed, and dreary November, with its leaden sky, made all without seem cheerless. The wind moaned dismally through the branches of the tamaracks at the door, and played at "hide and seek" among the leafless rose bushes. One day, after Lina had been more despondent than ever, and Juno, having finished her household duties, was sitting with folded hands, seemingly intent upon the gambols of a playful kitten; but in reality thinking of Lina and considering what she had best do, her mistress said:

"Juno, I wish to have a long talk with you."

This was just what Juno had long been wishing for, and she arose with alacrity and followed Lina into the little parlor, where a cheerful fire was burning on the hearth, which, with the heavy red curtains, served to give the room a cheerful appearance. The piano stood open, but no light fingers called forth its lively notes. Juno would open it every morning, saying, apologetically, "that it made the room look more pleasant-like, and more as if master Richard was home."

Lina seated herself in a large easy chair, while Juno took a seat on a low ottoman at her feet.

"Juno, I have never confided to you my early history. I have been thinking much of late, and have concluded to tell you all about myself." Whereupon she told Juno all the reader already knows, together with other facts which it is not our purpose at present to disclose.

"Juno," she continued, after a long silence, during which she had been toying with a beautiful ring on her third finger—it was Richard's gift, "I sometimes think I shall not live long, and, indeed, I should not wish to, if Richard never returns, for I could not live without him."

"Oh, my dear mistress Lina, don't talk that way! Master will come back! You must not talk of dying!" cried Juno, striving to keep back the tears that would fall in spite of all effort to restrain them.

"No, Juno, you cannot deceive me. I know that I cannot get well. You know my situation, and it is not best that you should be with me any longer alone. I wish you to engage the services of some competent old lady immediately. My marriage certificate and letters you will find in a little rose-wood box in my work-stand drawer. When I am gone, Juno, put this ring with the other things, and keep them carefully for my sake. If Richard ever comes home, you may give them to him. Tell him that though my heart was breaking, I loved him to the last. That is all now; I am tired and wish to sleep. You may stop at the post-office as you come through the village."

Juno was successful in finding an old lady of suitable qualifications. Old Mrs. Butterworth had just arrived by the Ruthford stage, and was one of those fat, motherly, smiling, rosy-cheeked old ladies that straightway win one's confidence. So home she went with Juno, who, though delighted with her success, did not forget to stop at the post-office.

The postmaster, from Juno's frequent visits and disappointed face, had learned to know her, and on this occasion hastened to produce and hand to the astonished woman a letter bearing the New Orleans postmark, and address to Mrs. Lina H. Tracy. Juno gave an exclamation of delight, as she thought of the joyful tidings she hoped to convey to the anxious, weary wife.

Lina was standing by the window when Juno and Mrs. Butterworth came up the walk, the former holding the letter triumphantly aloft. Lina sank nervous and trembling into a seat, as Juno rushed tumultuously into the room, exclaiming, "a letter from master Richard!" and could only articulate faintly, "Give it to me, Juno."

She glanced at the well-known superscription, and, with trembling hand, opened the fatal letter, to read the cruel words which would freeze the life from her young heart, and extinguish the life of the rapidly fading flower. Once, twice she read, with staring eyes, the words that closed her brief dream of happiness, when she fell heavily to the floor in a death-like swoon.

CHAPTER IX.   **April 22, 1865**

"Rest for the weary."

Mrs. Butterworth and Juno hastened to raise the insensible Lina, and lay her upon the sofa. The mischievous letter had fluttered from Lina's nerveless hand, and now lay quietly on the bright red carpet. Juno, with wise forethought, secured it, and then started in quest of the village physician, while Mrs. Butterworth used every effort to try and restore the pale creature who had already enlisted her warmest sympathy. Juno soon returned with the venerable Dr. Murdoch, who gravely shook his head, as he gazed on the sharp outlines of the deathlike face before him.

After awhile Lina opened her eyes wearily, looked from one to the other with a sadly bewildered air, and then, shudderingly, closed them again, ever and anon[1] murmuring, wildly, incoherent sentences, but seemed not to notice any one.

The daylight was fast waning. A gray November evening was ushered in. The tea-kettle was steaming over a cheerful fire in the bright little kitchen, and Juno was quietly preparing supper for the Doctor and Mrs. Butterworth. The lamps were lighted; the curtains drawn; the pet-kitten quietly dozed on the stool near the fire; all seemed cheerful and home-like.

After tea, all were seated around the couch of the sufferer; hour after hour sped by, and naught was heard save the heavy breathing of the invalid and the ticking of the little French clock upon the mantel, until after the little time-piece had chimed, in silvery tones, the hour of midnight; then, there were troubled faces, anxious whispers, and hurried steps, through the remaining hours of the night; and, when the cloudless morning dawned, a fair form was wrapped in the calm repose of death. Sweet Lina slept the dreamless sleep, the sleep that knows no waking here on earth. One of earth's weary ones—surely in heaven there is rest for such as thee. In the large easy chair, nestled amid its crimson depths, a beautiful babe was sleeping, a tender waif, cast motherless upon the sea of life. Poor little one, it would seem thou wert too fair and fragile to dwell in this cold world of ours! How striking the contrast between mother and child! The one had drooped and faded beneath the burden of life's trials until death released her weary spirit and she found rest; the other, sweet innocent, slept all unconscious of the great future. What trials were in store for that little one were wisely withheld.

Lina had lived long enough to kiss and bless her babe, and to whisper in the ear of Juno, to "call her Claire Neville Tracy. Be faithful to my child, Juno; never forsake her, and, as you may be faithful to her, my Father in heaven will reward you."

Poor Juno, with tearful eyes, promised all that Lina had required, and then, with choking voice, asked, "Have you not one word for Master Richard?" A beautiful smile lighted up her pale face, and she faintly whispered, "I love and—" but the sentence died on her lips; and, ere Juno relinquished the little hand, the lids had closed over eyes into which the misty shadows of death were fast stealing. "Such is life!"

Strange hands robed the form of the departed for the grave; strange but kind hands smoothed the shining curls, and placed the lovely snow-flowers on her meek bosom. Dr. Murdoch kindly superintended all arrangements for the funeral, which many of the warm-hearted villagers attended, and Lina was laid to rest on the bleak hill-side, where soon the pure, white snow would lie heavy on the lonely grave, and fierce northern winds would moan through the tall pines; but, when the Spring comes, fragrant roses and wild wood flowers would bloom until the chill Autumn blasts would rob them of their fleeting beauty.

Mrs. Butterworth remained to assist Juno in taking care of the baby, Claire, upon whom every care was bestowed. The little one grew, fair and rosy, and would open its great black eyes and try to look about, and soon learn to chirrup its delight when Juno's good-humored face crossed its infant vision, much to the satisfaction and encouragement of its kind nurses.

Thus the long dreary winter passed away, and a fitful New England March was on hand. Near the close of a pleasant afternoon Mrs. Butterworth and Juno were taking an early tea. Little Claire was sleeping in the cradle, her round cheeks rosy with the hue of health. A knock at the door arrested the flow of pleasant tea-table chat; Juno answered the summons, and was surprised at the unexpected vision of George Manville, who greeted her warmly and with smiling face.

"Where is Master Richard?" was Juno's first inquiry.

"In Europe, I suppose," was the immediate reply. "Did you not know it?"

"No!" said Juno, with astonishment. "What could have taken him to Europe without coming to see Miss Lina?" continued Juno, indignantly. "And that's just what killed her, poor thing!"

"Killed her!" ejaculated Manville, with pale face and aghast manner. "Did I understand you to say Mrs. Tracy was dead?" he asked with quivering lips.

"Yes, she is dead!" replied Juno. "And this is her child," said she, taking up little Claire, who had just awaked from her long afternoon nap.

Manville gazed long on the beautiful child which was a miniature likeness of his handsome and noble friend. What thoughts were passing through his brain it would be difficult to devise.

Mrs. Butterworth prepared supper for Manville, and, while discussing the merits of the same, he asked Juno what she intended doing. She could not tell, as she had still thought Richard would come back; but, now that he was not coming, she concluded to ask his advice.

Manville advised the sale of the cottage and furniture, the proceeds of which would enable her to live comfortably with little Claire, and then to remove to some other village. Juno acquiesced in this arrangement. So Manville took up his abode at the cottage, and undertook the management of affairs.

In a few days, Rose Cottage was advertised for sale; a gentleman and his daughter, seeing the advertisement, called to look at the cottage, and were so pleased with it, that, finding the furniture also was for sale, proposed to buy the cottage already furnished, which proposal just suited Manville, and pretty Rose Cottage became the home of Mr. Villars, who was a native of Vermont.

Addie Villars was delighted with every thing in and about the cottage; "O, papa!" she exclaimed, with animation, "such exquisite taste, such harmony of color in the arrangement of every thing; I know I should have loved Mrs. Tracy."

Mr. Villars smiled at his daughter's enthusiasm, saying, "that he did not doubt Mrs. Tracy was a very worthy person."

Addie decided that no change should be made in the disposition of the furniture, but that every thing should remain as it was.

After her mistress' death, Juno had taken scrupulous care to have every thing placed just as Lina used to arrange and loved to see them. And the result was that months later, when a pale, emaciated stranger stopped at the cottage, it wore the same appearance as when Richard and Lina were its happy occupants, and his apparent agitation drew tears of sympathy from the gentle Addie Villars, who, with the sad stranger, visited the lone grave on the hill side.

Mrs. Butterworth went home. A few weeks after, Juno, with the infant Claire, was snugly installed in a cozy little house many miles from her old home. Manville had taken particular care to have every thing arranged for her comfort and convenience. Juno was satisfied and grateful, and thought Manville very kind. But had she known the villainous heart masked by that faultless exterior, she could have formed a better estimate of his real character. And Richard, so deeply wronged, so basely deceived, should have known that "a man may smile and be a villain still."[2]

CHAPTER X.   **April 29, 1865**

Richard in New Orleans.

Soon after Richard's arrival in New Orleans he wended his way home. It was late in the afternoon. Colonel Tracy was seated on the verandah, reading, when Richard came up. "Good afternoon, father," he said, cheerfully extending his hand at the same time.

Colonel Tracy took no notice of the proffered hand, but exclaimed, angrily, "So sir, you have come to insult me with your presence! But follow me to the library, I wish not to quarrel with you here!"

Richard followed the choleric[1] old gentleman, as requested, into the library. Colonel Tracy closed and locked the door, to secure them from intrusion, then confronting his son, with threatening mien, said: "Now, sir, give an account of your proceedings; I want no evasion whatever, but a clear and concise statement of facts."

Richard related all that had transpired, from his first acquaintance with Lina to the present time: his betrothal on the Alhambra; the scene at the dinner table after Colonel Tracy's return from the plantation; Manville's purchase of the slave girl Lina, which was only a ruse, as Manville merely acted for his friend; the departure of the trio for the North; the quiet bridal at the little New England parsonage; Alfred Hays' departure; the purchase of Rose Cottage; and subsequent experiences for the Colonel's benefit, in his usual characteristic manner.

The Colonel's rage was without bounds, and he wrathfully exclaimed, "Oh! that a son of mine should thus disgrace himself and family, as to marry a negress—a slave—the illegitimate offspring of a spendthrift, a drunkard, and a libertine, a being sunk so low in the scale of humanity as to be unworthy the name of a man. It's awful! 'Tis abominable! Fool that you are, to allow yourself to be thus entrapped by a pretty face; and, no doubt, by this time you have wearied of your toy. If you have, it will be well, for as you are under age, your marriage is illegal, and, with the assistance of a trusty lawyer, its validity may be annulled. You can visit Europe a year or two, until the memory of this disgraceful affair has died out. I will settle an annuity on your—" he could not add the word *wife*. It would have choked him, so he corrected himself by saying, "on the girl, which will be sufficient to support her decently, and that is much better than she deserves, the artful wench, to palm herself off for a lady. Our society is getting into a pretty state, when the sons of the best families stoop to marry their fathers' slaves. You have imbibed the pernicious sentiments of northern demagogues until they have encompassed your ruin. What is to become of our institution, if we take our slaves upon an equality with ourselves? What slave on the plantation would properly respect you as their master, while they knew your wife was a negro slave— yes, worse than a slave? But to return to the point in question, will you renounce that girl? The way is perfectly clear, and the desired result may be arrived at with little difficulty. Of course it will cause some commotion in the 'upper circles,' and give your name an unpleasant notoriety for a season, but in the course of time that will wear away. As I said before, visit Europe a year or two, and when you return, there is not a young lady in New Orleans that would not accept your hand and fortune."

Colonel Tracy stopped abruptly and turned to his son, who sat erect, with livid face and flashing eyes, and with an air of such resolute determination that he felt very uncertain as to the impression produced by his reasoning, and he imperatively asked: "Well, sir, what is your decision?"

Richard possessed extraordinary power of self-control, and replied, in those calm, measured tones which always give such an advantage in an exciting discussion and voluntarily win the respect of an opponent, "Father, as much as I love and respect you, I cannot accede to a proposal that would so deeply involve my honor and integrity. I cannot forsake my wife. I did not win Lina's affections to basely deceive her, nor did I marry her to cruelly desert her. I would submit to any fate rather than become a party to such a degrading proceeding. I see no honorable avenue of escape, if I desired one, and I earnestly assure you I do not. Those pernicious sentiments, as you are pleased to term them, which I have imbibed at the North, only teach me to respect the rights of my fellow-citizens. Lina is not responsible for her unfortunate birth and surroundings. She is pure, refined, and good, has been educated far from the contaminating influence which southern society exerts over its followers. All else I can well overlook. I would not own a slave if I possessed the wealth of a Croesus.[2] The institution of slavery is of itself accursed, and will yet prove the fatal Nemesis[3] of the South, for do not think that a just God will allow any people so deeply wronged to go unavenged."

Colonel Tracy sat speechless with rage and astonishment, while Richard was speaking, and when he had finished he rose from his chair and confronting his son said: "Richard, if you persist in carrying out this unexampled piece of folly, I shall disinherit you. Not a penny of mine shall go to you or yours, and my doors shall ever be closed against you. Your mother and brother shall never acknowledge you as son and brother, and your name shall be as that of one who has slept a century in his tomb, uncared for and forgotten; so you can make your choice; you know the conditions."

"I cannot forsake my wife," was the firm, unfaltering reply. "Your judgment is severe, and—perhaps, it is just, but I will abide by it without murmuring."

"You dare to defy me!" yelled the Colonel, his face black with rage. "But I will conquer you yet! For I will see you die at my feet before you shall return to the arms of that accursed wife! Yes, I will kill you, and suffer hanging for it!" and drawing a pistol from his pocket took deliberate aim and fired.

Richard, having risen from his chair, exclaimed:

"Father, would you murder your own son!" and fell heavily to the floor, writhing in his own blood, the ball having entered his right side.

Hurrying feet were heard traversing the wide halls—the door was burst open, and Mrs. Tracy rushed into the library, closely followed by Manville, who had just returned, and hearing of Richard's arrival, had come direct to Colonel Tracy's, while groups of frightened negroes crowded the door and thronged the hall, presenting a weird scene, as the twilight shadows were now gathering.

Nellie Tracy gazed from the insensible form of her son to her husband, exclaiming, "Frank, O! Frank! May God forgive you! You have killed my child!" and then sunk fainting to the floor.

Colonel Tracy stood gazing upon the forms of his wife and son, with wild, glaring eyes. Manville alone possessed some presence of mind. He directed the negroes to take charge of their mistress, while he turned his attention to Colonel Tracy. "Come, my friend," he said, attempting to lead him from the library.

"Manville, I am perfectly sane; I know what I have done. Take that boy away, any where, out of my sight and hearing, for I care not whether he lives or dies."

Manville knew that the Colonel was in earnest, so he hailed a passing hack, and, with the assistance of the driver and several of the slaves, the wounded man was carefully placed in it, and driven slowly to a quiet private boarding-house, in a retired part of the city, while others were dispatched in quest of medical aid.

It would be impossible to attempt a description of Colonel Tracy's feelings. Indignation against Richard, and apprehension for his delicate wife, were the predominant workings of his soul. Mrs. Tracy was indeed in a critical state, and well might her passionate husband tremble for her safety. Through the long watches of the night great was the anxiety of that wretched man, for the life of his loved one hung, as it were, by a thread.

CHAPTER XI.   May 6, 1865

An equivocal friend.

Mrs. Lisle, the landlady of the private boarding house to which the insensible Richard was taken, was a widow of prepossessing appearance, and had evidently been in much better circumstances than at the present. She was kind-hearted, sensitive and refined. She was shocked, when Manville and his assistant brought the wounded man into the hall, and, in the glare of light, she saw the face of Richard so frightfully pale. But, knowing the necessity of immediate assistance, with the aid of Lettie, a little colored girl, she soon prepared a room and couch for the reception of Richard, at which time Dr. Singleton arrived, who, after a careful examination, pronounced Richard in a very critical state, his wound being a severe one; and, in falling, his head had grazed some heavy article of furniture, inflicting a severe bruise on the temple. With some difficulty, the hateful ball was extracted and the wound dressed; after which, Dr. Singleton prepared a solution, sleep-provoking in its nature, and Richard was comparatively comfortable for the night.

He slept quietly for several hours, when he became restless, moaning and murmuring sadly incoherent sentences; and, ere the morning dawned, Dr. Singleton, who had made an early visit, found his patient much worse; the scarlet cheeks, parched lips, heated breath, and wildly beating pulse, betokening the presence of the fever he so much dreaded.

"This is bad, Mrs. Lisle, very bad," he remarked: "I feared this. He has been quite delirious through the night, you say?" he asked, while preparing the necessary medicines.

"Yes!" replied Mrs. Lisle, "he has talked alternately of his mother, of Lina, and an enraged father. I think it is a family quarrel; but, from the confused and disconnected nature of his raving, I could not, of course, determine the exact nature of the trouble."

At this moment, Richard moved uneasily, and murmured quite audibly, "Lina, he will not forgive me! But we will live for each other now, darling! It was so cruelly unjust to attempt to take you from me!" A pause, and then in a pitifully pleading voice, "Lina, don't leave me; it is all dark and lonely here."

Dr. Singleton leaned over his patient, and placing his cool hand upon Richard's heated brow, spoke to him in calm soothing tones. The pleading glance of those bright, dark eyes, went straight to the doctor's heart: for he too had been a father, and his only child, a young man of Richard's age, had been suddenly stricken down in a foreign land—had died among strangers, and was buried upon the banks of the beautiful Rhine.[1]

The Doctor was thinking of all this, as he gazed with compassion upon the unconscious youth, when Richard exclaimed in ringing tones, "You will not take my beautiful Lina from me! What matters it, if her skin is dark, if the blood of the despised race tinges her veins? Oh! believe me, she is good and pure! Oh! you must save her! You will not, must not let them take her!"

The Doctor stood somewhat aghast! What was the solution of this strange language? To what did the unconscious sufferer allude? Could it be, that he was given to one of the popular vices of southern society? One glance at his patient, and he was re-assured. Dissipation had not placed its foul mark upon that fresh beardless face, surrounded by clustering, black curls. No, the stigma of vice had not attached itself to that noble youth! The Doctor felt this, and determined to befriend the young man whose acquaintance he was forming under such peculiar circumstances, and who, he believed, was worthy of his deepest sympathy.

Thus, Richard unconsciously won for himself a warm friend— one who was destined greatly to influence his after life; and thus it is, in life, we sometimes unconsciously win friendship, while we fail, signally, when earnestly striving to gain and retain it.

Soon after Dr. Singleton took his leave, Manville appeared, refreshed and smiling, from a fresh toilette and an excellent breakfast. Mrs. Lisle was prepossessed in the young man's favor. He seemed so thoughtful of his friend's comfort—so anxious to alleviate his sufferings, that she willingly resigned her position as nurse, for the present, in favor of Manville, while she went to look after her various household duties.

As the days passed, Richard continued to grow worse, and Dr. Singleton's visits more frequent and prolonged. Mrs. Lisle spent many hours by the couch of the sufferer, while Manville devoted his entire time to nursing his friend. As the weeks passed slowly by, Richard's spirit fluctuated between life and death, while his voice might be heard sometimes in ringing tones, and at other times, in almost sobbing wail, imploring the imaginary Lina not to forsake him.

At last the crisis was passed, and Richard was convalescent. Dr. Singleton was fairly jubilant when able to pronounce his patient out of danger. As soon as Richard was permitted to converse with any one, he asked Manville, in the absence of Dr. Singleton and Mrs. Lisle, if he had written to Lina concerning his illness. Manville was unprepared for this question. He had not thought of it, and inwardly blamed himself for his stupidity, in not being prepared for this emergency; as it was, he could only admit the truth, he had not; and his eyes fell beneath Richard's glance, so full of reproach and indignation.

"Oh, George, how could you be so careless, not to use a harsher term? Such forgetfulness is really criminal. It will kill my wife, not to hear from me through all these long weeks, and not understanding the cause of this strange silence. It was cruelly unkind to forget her. Poor Lina, I know your little heart is breaking." He was growing restless and excited. "George, you must write for me immediately; bring ink and paper to my bedside, and write, while I dictate." Manville did as requested, and the blank sheet was soon filled with kind and loving words from Richard. He spoke guardedly of his illness, and every allusion that would have had the slightest tendency to alarm his wife, was anxiously suppressed. "I shall be home soon," he kindly remarked, "when, I hope, we shall part no more!" How thoughtful of her, his only care! Kind and encouraging messages were also sent to Juno.

After the letter was finished, Richard said, excitedly, "Now read it for me, George Manville! Read it to the end! That will do," he said with a sigh of satisfaction and sunk back upon his pillow, wearily closing his eyes; while Manville, who promised to mail the letter immediately, passed out, and, proceeding direct to his sleeping apartment, lighted a small silver lamp, drew the letter, around which cling so many hopes and fears, from an inner pocket, gazed upon it a few seconds, scornfully curling his lips, and, a sinister light flashing from his eyes, held it over the ruthless blaze until the curled, crisp embers fell at his feet, exclaimed exultingly, "So perish all your dreams of happiness!"

CHAPTER XIII.   May 20, 1865

The Tracy's.

On the morning following the tragic event before narrated, Colonel Tracy was pacing his room like a caged lion. His wife, his idolized Nellie, was ill, perhaps dying, while he was rigidly excluded from her presence. And if she died, he was her murderer. Oh, the agony of thought! What of Richard? He resolutely tried to banish all thoughts of his son, but despite every effort, the vision of that pale, noble face, passed before him. And these last words in ringing tones, "Father, would you murder your own son?" haunted his memory. He seemed to hear them still. Was he, indeed, the murderer of his son? This question presented itself many times. His reflections were sad, and bitter. He half-expected a visit or message from Manville, but received neither. His anxiety for his wife increased as hours passed, and the invariable reply of the attendants as they passed to and from his wife's chamber, "No better, Massa" grated harshly upon his ear. This suspense was unendurable, he would bear it no longer. At this moment Mattie, the nurse, entered the room. Colonel Tracy scarcely vouchsafed a single glance upon the pink-faced, black-eyed baby she respectfully presented, but asked almost fiercely, "How is my wife?" "Very bad, Massa," replied the woman, sadly. For days Mrs. Tracy's life was despaired of, and through those days of awful uncertainty, Colonel Tracy was constant in his care of baby Belle. Next to his wife, his every thought was of her. He almost idolized the little black-eyed stranger, and much of that idolatry clung to him through life. Belle was always her father's favorite, and right royally did the little beauty queen it over her father's heart.

But Nellie Tracy did not die. Slowly she struggled back to partial health, but so changed, so faded, a mere semblance of her former self. Her husband followed her like a shadow, anticipating her every wish, doing every thing in the most kind and gentle manner, evincing by a thousand little acts of thoughtful kindness how dear she was to him. Nellie was pleased and grateful to her husband, but this was not what she needed to bring perfect health to the dropping figure, roses to the pale cheek, and the light of happiness to the brown eyes which revealed such a world of sadness in their liquid depths. Richard, her first born pride, her noble son: it was of him she longed to know, yet dared not ask. And her husband never alluded to his son. Colonel Tracy, perhaps, with a view of remedying the true evil, proposed a visit to Italy. Nellie faintly acquiesced, but ere their departure, she gained through Mattie the intelligence that Richard was living. That was all, but she felt better and improved perceptibly, and with a slight semblance of cheerfulness watched the busy preparation for departure. Mattie, the nurse, went with them to take charge of baby Belle and Little Lloyd. Mattie was shrewd and intelligent, and Nellie, in poor health as she was, could not trust her children to the care of a stranger, and Mattie had nursed and loved little Richard even as she now loved little Lloyd and Isabelle. Nellie always found a ready and sympathetic listener in her faithful attendant, when talking of her son.

Long years the Tracys were absent from New Orleans. And many times they were near, *very* near a sad, thoughtful-browed man, who was rarely known to smile, and would stand up as if spell-bound, in the mammoth hotels, gazing upon the register where one line claimed his attention, (*Colonel Tracy and wife, nurse and two children*). Were they indeed so near him? His heart bounded when he thought of his gentle mother. He would see her and talk to her. But then came the bitter memory of his father's curse. No, he would not seek her, but all unknown to them, he would at least look upon her fair face. One evening little Lloyd was seated with half-closed eyes upon the sofa in the nurse's room waiting for Mattie to return and put him to bed. He was suddenly clasped by a pair of stout arms. Warm kisses fell on cheek, brow and lips. The wondering child opened his eyes wide and looked up into the sad face above him with a confiding smile. A few moments more he was soundly sleeping, upon the stranger's bosom. Richard strained the little fellow convulsively to his heart. His thoughts were busy with the past,—time passed unheeded. Mattie entered the room, unconscious of the surprise that awaited her. An exclamation more vehement than elegant escaped the astonished woman as her eyes fell upon Richard.

"Oh! Massa Richard, dear Massa, I'm so glad to see you," and poor Mattie fairly broke down from her excess of joy, threw her apron over her head and wept like a child. Richard was deeply affected by Mattie's expression of feeling, and, waiting till she became calmer, asked for his father and mother. Mattie related all that had transpired. Richard was visibly affected when Mattie spoke of his mother's ill health, and her anxiety concerning him. He hastily traced a few lines upon a leaf from his diary, handed them to Mattie, and said, "Give them to mother," and he hesitated a moment. "If I could look upon my mother, if for only one moment, I would be so thankful." He looked wistfully in Mattie's face; she divined his wish. "Follow me," she said, leading the way to Mrs. Tracy's room. They entered with noiseless step. Nellie was calmly sleeping, her brown hair swept back from the pale forehead: perhaps in her dreams she felt his loved presence, for the sweet lips wreathed in a beautiful smile. Richard, with tearful eyes kneeled by her couch and prayed such a prayer as the angels love to listen to, and the effect of that fervent humble prayer was felt by Nellie Tracy. Even in her sleep a holy smile rested upon her features. Richard arose, pressed one long, loving kiss upon his mother's lips, and passed from the room with Mattie.

"Oh! Mattie, be kind and faithful to mother." He pressed a piece of gold into her hand and was gone, just in time to avoid a meeting with Colonel Tracy, who was returning from a dinner party. The next morning Mrs. Tracy said to Mattie, "I dreamed such a beautiful dream! I thought Richard was here, I seem to feel his kiss upon my lips yet." Mattie made no reply but gave her Richard's note, which read as follows:

DEAR MOTHER:
With the deepest sorrow I learned from Mattie of your failing health. —Have no anxiety about me; I have suffered much. Perhaps we will meet no more on earth, but I am looking forward to a happy reunion in heaven.

Your loving son,
RICHARD.

Mr. Villars and Addie were interested in their guest and rendered him every attention. After he had paid a visit to the lone grave on the hillside where sweet wild flowers were blooming, it was late ere he returned and Addie heard, until the morning light dawned, the unbroken steps of Richard as he walked his room with steady and unceasing tread. At breakfast he looked pale and care worn. "Miss Addie, will you accompany me this morning to visit my wife's grave?" Addie kindly assented, and together they visited the grave.

"Would you, Miss Addie, grant me one favor if I ask it?"

"Certainly," replied his companion.

"Thank you! It is this—will you sometimes visit Lina's grave when I am gone, it will be so lonely on this hillside. I cannot bear the thought that none should visit her last resting place."

Addie promised and nobly did she fulfil her promise. Richard left them with many thanks for their kindness. And, as years passed, Mr. Villars and Addie spoke often of Richard, and Addie wondered if he would ever return to Rose Cottage.

CHAPTER XIV.   May 27, 1865

Claire and Isabelle.

Isabelle Tracy was alone in her luxuriously furnished boudoir; curtains of light and elegant material shaded the windows, so that a soft voluptuous light pervaded the silent apartment. A carpet, adorned with large roses, upon a delicate white ground, covered the floor. Chairs and divans, elegant and expensive, were disposed about the room in charming negligence; rare old paintings and exquisite engravings adorned the walls, bespeaking rare artistic taste in the beautiful owner. Between the windows a perfect cataract of lace fell on either side of an elegant toilet table, prettily hiding a collection of beautiful cups, flagons, boxes and vases, containing rare perfumes and pomades, as curious as costly. Of what was Isabelle thinking, as she sat with contracted brow, flashing eyes, and compressed lips, while a crimson spot burned on each cheek, and her white hands were clasped and unclasped in a sort of mechanical, absent-minded manner? At last, giving expression to her thoughts, she said: "Who and what is this Claire Neville, whose striking resemblance to myself is already the theme of conversation with every body? O, I hate her, with her queenly air and stately walk! Her beauty, they say, is almost marvelous. Can it be possible that she surpasses me in loveliness?" And Isabelle stood before the faithful mirror, which reflected a fair face, striking in its singular beauty. Eagerly she scrutinized every feature: the brilliant, almond-shaped black eyes, with curving, black brows and sweeping silken lashes; the small mouth, which rivaled a half-blown rose in its dewy loveliness, displaying rows of even, pearl-white teeth; the soft, oval cheeks, now flushed with excitement, and the crowning attraction, a wealth of beautiful black hair, which rippled in curling waves to her slender waist.

As she continued to gaze a smile of satisfaction wreathed her lovely lips. What had she to fear from the self-possessed governess? She pulled the bell-cord, and in a few moments her summons was answered by a trim-looking mulatto girl.

"Mira, you may dress me now," she said.

While Mira was selecting the proper articles of dress, Isabelle resumed, "I wish you to dress my hair with great care this afternoon. You have not forgotten the new style you learned from the French hair-dresser?"

"Oh no, Miss," was Mira's quick reply, as she separated her mistress' long, shining hair, and with nimble fingers plaited beautiful braids to take the place of the straggling tresses.

The task being completed, Isabelle, with a gratified smile, said, "Mira, you have indeed succeeded well, and you shall be suitably rewarded."

When Isabelle was pleased she was exceedingly gracious. Before descending to the parlor, she turned to take another look in the mirror, and surveyed with ill-concealed pride her beautiful face and magnificent figure.

Count Sayvord, who was lounging about the parlor, advanced to greet her. "You are looking fair, *my belle*," he said, with a courtly bow. Isabelle rewarded him with a most fascinating smile.

Count Sayvord possessed rare conversational powers. He had read much and travelled a great deal, and was also a close observer of human nature, and the manners and customs of the different people he had been among.

An hour passed, and the handsome ormula[1] clock upon the mantel chimed four. A shadow rested upon Isabelle's brow. This was the hour for the children to take their music lesson.

Claire was a perfect model of punctuality and precision. Isabelle knew this, and thought, "now for an infliction of that everlasting governess. If she was only safe in the land of 'steady habits,'[2] I would willingly be responsible for the education of a dozen little sisters." As a realization of her fears, the musical voice of Claire was heard in the distance, in company with Laura and Nellie.

A peculiar expression passed over the Count's face, as he noticed the too visible vexation of his companion. Perhaps he understood, and perhaps he did not.

The trio entered the parlor. Claire acknowledged the presence of the Count and Isabelle by a graceful inclination of the head, and passed on. Sayvord continued his conversation with Isabelle, but his eyes continually wandered to where Claire sat, instructing her young charge. He was mystified in a chaos of doubt and perplexities. Who was this unassuming and stately Claire? Whenever he thought of Claire, she was strangely associated with the tall, dark stranger he had met years before at his uncle Clayburn Sayvord's residence. He also observed that Claire was an object of deep interest to Lloyd and Colonel Tracy, and it was quite evident, whatever the mystery was, that they were also puzzled to account for the resemblance between Claire Neville and Isabelle Tracy. Those two, so very like in appearance, yet so unlike in disposition.

Sayvord answered Isabelle's questions with the air of one whose thoughts are far otherwise engaged. She noticed this, and was almost ready to openly resent it. To crown all, the Count excused himself, and wended his way to the arbor, to enjoy a quiet siesta, and, perhaps, to dream of the beautiful governess. Ah, Count Sayvord, unraveling the mystery that envelopes a beautiful woman is dangerous business.

Isabelle was angry. Was the Count becoming infatuated with that detested governess? What subtle charm did she cast about her? Lloyd had eyes, but he could see no one but Claire. And now Sayvord was about to follow his example. Her father, too, was unaccountably drawn towards the young stranger, while the negroes gazed after her with wonder, and talked mysteriously of somebody and something, with extra variations in the way of (not very pretty) grimaces and significant glances, and all the *elite* of New Orleans became suddenly interested in the health and welfare of their charming friend, Miss Tracy.

Carriages could be seen at all hours before the aristocratic mansion of the Tracys. Isabelle understood perfectly the curiosity, and, in not a few cases, the animosity which prompted these solicitous visits. "This is becoming unendurable," she murmured. "I must speak to papa," and she darted a haughty glance at the unconscious Claire, who was the innocent cause of all this commotion.

Claire was warmly attached to her young pupils, and they improved rapidly under her gentle tuition. Mrs. Tracy loved her with almost maternal affection, and Claire, poor, motherless Claire, repaid her by every kind and loving attention affection could devise. Lloyd regarded her as he would a favorite sister. He noticed his sister's antipathy towards her and sought to render every thing pleasant. Claire felt his natural goodness of heart, and was less reserved with him than with others. She would, while in his presence, cast aside her dignity and become for a little while her own charming self. He never wearied gazing upon her fair face, which shadowed forth the innocent heart beneath, and always felt more happy while in her company. Sayvord envied his friend the pleasure of the governess' society.

CHAPTER XV.   June 3, 1865

The Veiled Picture.

In the soft, early twilight, Mrs. Tracy and Claire sat hand in hand. For a long while neither spoke, but a subdued expression rested upon the face of each. Mrs. Tracy passed her hand caressingly over Claire's glossy braids, and murmured softly,

"Sweet Claire, you know not half how dear you are to me. I have learned to think I could not live, bereft of your presence. There is something in your voice and manner that draws me irresistibly towards you, and I hope you will never think of leaving me."

"Dear Mrs. Tracy," replied Claire, her sweet voice tremulous with emotion, "it would be unkind, as well as ungrateful, for me to leave you. I have no mother to care for me, no home where kind and loving friends impatiently endure my absence, and anxiously await my return. You have been kind, very kind, to me, and I already love you as a dear mother, and you have taught me how great was my loss in never knowing one whom I possessed a right to call by the blessed name of mother. You have been kind in allowing me to love you," and the proud Claire, who was cold and indifferent to all others, was weeping bitterly, her proud head pillowed upon Nellie Tracy's gentle breast, who talked in low, soft tones, tender and endearing words, until Claire was soothed, and lay like a weary child, her large, tender eyes resting with a dreamy expression upon Mrs. Tracy's pale, placid face.

"Claire, I will tell you of my married life. I have suffered, God alone knows how deeply. I could not confide my history to an indifferent person, but with your kind, sensitive heart, I know you will sympathize with me."

Claire's eyes were full of interest, and, as Mrs. Tracy proceeded, she drew instinctively nearer, her crimson lips apart, and the color deepening and fading from her cheeks. She was strangely interested in the fate of Richard and his slave bride. What was there in that history, sad though it was, to make the blood thrill through her veins and her heart to throb almost painfully? When Mrs. Tracy finished speaking, Claire pressed her hand fondly, and imprinted a warm kiss upon her white brow, which delicate manifestation fully expressed her beautiful sympathy.

"Claire, dear, you remind me, in a thousand ways, of my poor absent son. Your face, voice, and manner, are so like his, that I almost fancy he is speaking to me through you. It is a foolish fancy, perhaps, but I have dreamed that a nearer and stronger tie than mere friendship, bound us together. This strange resemblance first enlisted my affection for you, but I love you for yourself alone, since I have learned to know your gentle heart."

The two, so strangely yet strongly attached, conversed long. Claire repaid her friend's confidence by giving a history of her lonely and almost friendless childhood. Mrs. Tracy listened with breathless interest, and it was quite evident her thoughts were busy with the past.

"Stay with me always, Claire, and you shall never again sigh for a mother's love."

Gratefully the great, sad eyes were lifted to her face, and Claire murmured her thanks in a low tone. After a pause, she said:

"You spoke of Richard's picture. If you would only let me see it," and her voice was singularly pleading.

"I am pleased that I can gratify you," replied Mrs. Tracy. "The old library has been unopened for years, except when visited by myself. The picture is veiled. I have one of the keys; the other was unaccountably lost. But you can take mine. You must be careful not to be seen visiting the library by Col. Tracy, or any one of the servants. He has forbidden any one to visit the library, and should any of the negroes observe your visit, they would not fail to report the same to him, and he would be greatly displeased." Gentle Nellie Tracy stood somewhat in awe of her lordly husband. "If you are not timid, to-night, after all have retired, would be the best time. I always go about midnight, and if you desire it, I will go with you."

Claire was pleased, and thanked her. Together they sat, sometimes silent, sometimes conversing in low tones, until the great bell in an adjoining yard tolled the hour of twelve. Mrs. Tracy arose, handed Claire a small lamp, took a large key from a private drawer, and prepared to lead the way to the old library.

Lightly they sped along the dark halls, streaked here and there by the pale yellow moonbeams. Arriving at the door, they listened breathlessly, until assured they were unobserved, and then inserted the key. The door was with difficulty unlocked, and swung back upon its hinges with a dull, grating sound. Claire looked around with blanched face and frightened air. Mrs. Tracy reassured her with a smile that fell athwart the gloomy apartment like a ray of bright sunlight. Mrs. Tracy closed and locked the door after them, and withdrawing the key, laid it on the heavy oaken desk. The key once withdrawn, the little guard fell over the keyhole with a sharp click, totally excluding every ray of light from penetrating the great, rambling hall without.

Mrs. Tracy drew aside the veil, and together they stood before the picture that seemed lifelike and breathing in the flickering, uncertain light of the small lamp. The handsome face seemed to smile down serenely upon those two women, who gazed upon it with such deep emotion. Claire's eyes were riveted upon that striking face. Eagerly she drank in its dark, noble beauty, with quivering lips and flushed cheeks. What awful mystery was it, at which she vainly clutched, and as vainly sought to unravel? Mrs. Tracy gazed attentively upon the two faces, which seemed an exact counterpart of each other. Her eyes rested first upon her son and then upon the beautiful, trembling girl at her side. Claire turned, their eyes met. One earnest, searching glance, and they read each other's thoughts. Claire exclaimed, excitedly:

"Mrs. Tracy, who am I? Oh, that face has haunted me in my dreams since my earliest recollection! Can it be that—?"

The sentence died upon her pale lips. A cautious step was heard traversing the hall. Nearer, nearer, it came, and slowly approached the library door, and stopped. A key turned in the lock, the door swung heavily back, and the affrighted women stood face to face with Col. Tracy, whose pale, haggard face bespoke great mental suffering. The trio gazed upon each other with equal consternation.

Chapter XVI.   **June 10, 1865**

Remorse.

Our readers, no doubt, are asking, what has become of Col. Tracy? With your permission we will invade the colonel's sanctuary, or, as Lloyd called the *new* library, "Pa's Retreat." Col. Tracy sits in the huge arm-chair, and bright, joyous sunbeams streaming in at the west windows fall warmly on the once raven locks, now closely threaded with silver. The little sunbeam all unnoticed, slides slowly down, and at last rests, quivering, deepening and fading upon the bright carpets. The colonel is thinner and paler than when we first knew him. His proud form is slightly bowed, and his searching, black eyes have an eager, restless, glance that but too truly betokens a mind ill at ease.

The colonel is living under a shadow, and has lived under it for years. But the iron will, the over-weening pride, which gave him strength to do and dare all things, was fast giving way, and the proud man felt as we all must feel some time: he was growing old.

How vain were all his vast possessions, as long as they failed to bring him *happiness*. Yes, there was the great secret. He had lived in vain. He had buoyed himself up with the belief that he was happy, while all the time the knowledge of ruin was nestled like a canker worm at his heart. But he had resolutely banished all thought of that one dark epoch in his life's history.

The colonel had become strangely unlike himself of late. He was unusually taciturn when in the presence of his family, and spent hours alone in his retreat, communing with his own sad thoughts. He would allow his mind to wander far back through the dim shadowy vista of the past, which was thronged with accusing spirits.

Remorseless memory dragged to light those scenes he had been for years striving to forget. Long silenced conscience was doing her work, and *remorse*, if not *penitence*, was fast tugging at the heart-strings of the stubborn old man. He groaned aloud, and perspiration bathed the pale brow, and saturated the heavy masses of hair.

"Why is it," he exclaimed excitedly, "the pale face of Claire Neville haunts my sleeping and waking hours, follows me like an avenging spirit? Her voice and smile madden me. Fool that I am to allow myself to be thus imprisoned." And the colonel made a desperate but vain attempt to rally his spirits.

"This is more than useless," he exclaimed. "Oh, Richard, my son! my son! my punishment is indeed greater than I can bear! A thousand times have I bitterly execrated that deed. My *curse* has recoiled upon my own head. Oblivion would be a heaven, but even that is denied me." He bowed his head upon his hands, as if to shut out the horrid picture that would present itself to his perturbed imagination. What was it to the guilty, wretched man, if the beautiful sunbeams deepened and faded, if the birds sang cheerily, and the flowers diffused their rich fragrance throughout the apartment? What was it to him if the wealth of mind, of poet, sage and statesman, loomed above him? He heeded not the setting sun, as the rays of his glory departed, and were hid behind a bank of gold and purple clouds. He heeded not the rosy twilight, freighted with the chirpings of myriads of insects. And all unheeded, the little stars came trooping forth, and pale Phoebus[1] shed her mellow rays upon all God's creatures. The high and lowly, the happy and miserable, the good and wicked, alike shared her beneficence. Truly the hour of retribution comes to all.

Hours passed unheeded, the conscience stricken man sat motionless, absorbed in grief. Years had passed since he had looked upon his son. Strange, that he had never thought to visit the picture in the old library. Years had passed since he had crossed the blood-stained threshold. An irresistible inclination to visit that picture seemed to take possession of him. Yes, he would go. But it seemed very like weakness. He did not wish to be observed visiting the old library, which the negroes regarded with superstitious dread and conversed in suppressed whispers as they passed it. No, it would not do to allow any one to know of this visit, and as a safe-guard against unpleasant comments, he concluded to wait until the inmates of the household were buried in slumber, then, unobserved, wend his way to the library.

Music, mirth, and laughter were wafted to his ears on the night air, from the parlors. Evidently there was no sorrow there. At length the songs and laughter were hushed. He heard the "Good-night," spoken in many tones, as the group in the parlor separated for the night. He waited an hour longer, and taking a small lamp, with cautious steps, threaded his way through the shadowy halls. It was rather humiliating to be stealing through his own house like a thief, at midnight. He cautiously approached the door, paused, and listened; he thought—was almost certain that he heard voices within. Listening a moment longer, and hearing nothing, he thought it only a freak of his perturbed imagination. Inserting his key in the lock, with one effort the heavy oaken door swung back, disclosing to his astonished gaze, his wife and Claire Neville standing before the veiled picture, their faces white with terror. What had brought these two women to the blood-stained library, at that hour? Again, the likeness of Claire Neville to his son, arrested his attention. He gazed alternately, with staring eyes upon the portrait of Richard, and the pale, trembling girl. It must be; it must be, he muttered, half audibly; but the proof, the proof.

Mrs. Tracy, from weakness and excessive fright, had fainted, and now rested like a broken lily upon Claire's bosom, who turned her imploring gaze upon Colonel Tracy, and said: "For the love of heaven take your wife; I fear this fright will kill her."

CHAPTER XVIII.   June 24, 1865

Dr. Singleton at Work.

After a lapse of eighteen years we renew our acquaintance with the somewhat eccentric, but worthy son of Aesculapius,[1] Dr. Singleton. The doctor is slightly changed during these long years, and presents a pleasing picture of healthy old age. His white hair is swept back from a brow somewhat furrowed by arduous labors, constant study, and the passage of years, which have all left a greater or less impression. But his eagle eye retains its wonted fire, and his powerful mind the vigor of his youthful days. The doctor is as genial as in the olden time. He has no skeleton which he seeks to hide from the gaze of all others, and which he himself looks upon with a strange fascination and horrid dread. The doctor is very popular, and his professional services are in great demand.

During many visits to various patients, he heard the all-absorbing topic of the day fully discussed and commented upon. Col. Tracy's Yankee governess had created a great sensation throughout the upper circles. Once, too, he caught a slight glimpse of the sweet, fair face, as he was hurriedly whirled past Col. Tracy's carriage, in which were seated Col. Tracy's children and their governess. That pale, sad face brought in its wake the memory of *another* face, patient and suffering. He turned and looked eagerly after the carriage, which, with its burden of youth and beauty, was fast retreating in the distance.

"I must know more of that young lady," he mentally decided. He discovered that the governess was the prevailing subject under discussion. Dame Rumor and Madam Gossip vied with each other in furnishing a proper solution to the inexplicable problem. The old doctor said nothing, but carefully noting the opinion of the masses, was able to form an *idea* of his own, and, with his usual acuteness, was very nearly correct.

"Now," said he, "if I could get trace of Manville, I think I could solve this mystery. If not by direct inquiry, perhaps by strategy I could gain the necessary information. I must make inquiry concerning his whereabouts."

The doctor was one of those with whom to *think* is to *act*. He immediately ordered dinner, after which, donning his hat and gloves, he sallied forth upon his tour of observation, and hoped for discovery. He knew that Manville had gradually degenerated from a gentlemanly coxcomb[2] into a confirmed *roue*.[3] He had often noticed the flushed and dim eyes of Manville, who passed him with unsteady step and shrinking eye. But it had been a long while now, since he had seen or heard any thing of Manville. The doctor, with a zeal worthy of him, made inquiry in various directions without eliciting the desired information. The old gentleman was not to be discouraged, but pertinaciously questioned every one whom he thought knew aught of Manville. He visited the haunts of vice and dissipation, with the hope of being able to hear something, but in vain.

Weeks passed, and he had failed as yet in gaining the desired knowledge. But tardy fortune at last smiled upon him. He learned, from a low, hired trader, that Manville had been seriously wounded, while intoxicated, at one of the fashionable restaurants and gambling saloons that infest the Crescent City, and was now slowly dragging out the remainder of his life, a miserable cripple, with the attending horrors of an accusing conscience.

The doctor lost no time in searching out his former acquaintance. In a dilapidated old building, far out of the city, Dr. Singleton found George Manville, the once handsome, gay, reckless, and iniquitous young man, *now* prematurely old, and trembling upon the verge of the grave, his mind assailed by a myriad of torturing thoughts, and the great wrong he had done Richard Tracy was not the least.

He was attended by an indifferent mulatto girl, who promptly answered all the doctor's queries, and conducted him without ceremony to Manville's apartment, which was sadly in need of a regenerating spirit.

Manville looked annoyed, as the bustling old gentleman proceeded to throw open the small windows and doors that a current of fresh air might penetrate the squalid room.

"You are dying, man, for the want of pure air! You must have air, and plenty of it, too, or you will not live a week! This is murder, nothing short of murder! Who is your medical advisor?"

This question was followed by a dozen others, all asked in one breath, and before Manville had time to answer the first. The doctor then turned his attention to Manville, and found indeed, that there was no hope of his recovery. The sick man was conscious of his state, and was at times perfectly indifferent to his fate. Again he seemed terrified by the visions his perturbed imagination conjured up. On the day of the doctor's visit, he was comparatively quiet. The old gentleman restrained his curiosity, and did not ask any questions during his first visit, but tried to render the sick man comfortable, and to put him at his ease in his presence, which it was quite evident he was far from feeling.

Every day Dr. Singleton wended his way out of the city, and might be seen entering the dilapidated old building. The sick room soon appeared to far greater advantage, for under the doctor's direction, Elynthia[4] had effected a most wonderful change.

Manville had learned to like the eccentric old gentleman, whose quaint speeches and genial smile dispelled a portion of the gloom that surrounded him, and he watched eagerly for the hour that would bring the promised visit. He grew weaker and weaker as the sultry days passed, and the doctor thought it was not best to delay the subject any longer, and one afternoon, when Manville seemed somewhat lively, after a few introductory remarks, he said:

"Manville, do you ever hear of Richard Tracy? I have found his child, and wish to find means of communicating with him."

CHAPTER XIX.   July 1, 1865

A Summons.

With a wildly beating heart, Claire wended her way to the library, where Col. Tracy impatiently awaited her. When she entered he greeted her with a strange blending of tenderness and formality. Claire sunk trembling into one of the huge chairs which was extending its kindly arms towards her. She glanced at the Colonel. He looked pale, and the hard lines about the proud mouth had strangely softened, and an inquiring light beamed from his dark eyes, as he bent them searchingly upon the face of the young girl. After taking several rapid turns across the library, he seated himself where he could obtain a full view of Claire's face, and said:

"Miss Neville, the striking resemblance which you bear to members of my family has deeply interested me, and created the desire to know something of your parents and early life. Do not hesitate to tell me," he said, encouragingly, "it is from purely disinterested motives that I seek this information. Sad events have transpired in my family in years passed, and a clear, concise statement of facts in relation to your parentage and childhood may serve to throw light upon several little circumstances which have always proved inexplicable to me."

Claire colored painfully as she felt that she must confess the humiliating truth. She knew nothing of her parents, not even their names. It was a comparatively easy matter to speak of this to Mrs. Tracy, but to talk with the stern old colonel was quite another thing. She, however, summoned sufficient courage to reply.

"What I know of my friendless, lonely childhood, I will willingly tell you, but of my parents I know nothing. I was raised by a colored nurse, who lives a few miles from the village of L—. I lived a wild, joyous life until my twelfth year, when I was placed at L— Seminary to be educated, at the expense of a stranger. True, the gentleman had been in the habit of visiting Juno at long intervals, and talking mysteriously of me, and sometimes talking of someone whom they called Richard. (Col. Tracy moved a little nearer to Claire.) The gentleman was handsome, tall, and dark. He often tried to win my confidence, but I shrank instinctively from him. His handsome face was repulsive in the extreme. For a long time I did not even know his name. At the last visit he paid Juno before I was placed at the Seminary, he dropped a handkerchief, which bore on one corner the name of—"

"Who?" interrupted the colonel, totally unable to be silent longer.

"George Manville!" continued Claire, "I kept the handkerchief and have always thought he was in some way connected with my parents."

"I thought so, I thought so!" said the colonel excitedly. Then turning to Claire, he asked: "How long is it since you saw George Manville?"

"Six years ago, this spring."

"Would you know him again?"

"His face seems stamped upon my memory."

"I am glad of that, for George Manville lives in New Orleans, and you shall see him, and perhaps learn something of your parents. By the way, have you no little memento or keepsake that belonged to your father or mother?"

"Only this," sliding a beautiful little ring, Juno's parting gift, from her finger, and handing it to Col. Tracy.

The initials "*R.T. to L.*" seemed to be engraved in letters of fire. "This was your mother's?" he said, inquiringly.

"It was," replied Claire, "Juno gave it to me just before I started south."

"Juno must know all about your parents," said the colonel, as he finished examining, and returned the glittering ring.

"She does," replied Claire, "but she would never tell me any thing in regard to them. I remember she was greatly excited when she learned that I was to be governess in your family, and said, 'What would Master Richard say of your going to be governess in that proud family?' I asked who Richard was, and importuned her, as I had many times before, to tell me who my parents were. But, as on all similar occasions, she remained obstinately silent. My resemblance to your daughter first excited Mr. and Mrs. Harrington's astonishment, who, as many others here, thought that I must be a relative of the family."

"Your appearance certainly verifies the supposition, and it may be proved that those suppositions are correct. One thing is certain, we must find George Manville, and obtain the knowledge we wish from him. It will be necessary to see Juno in the course of our investigation. I am somewhat apprehensive of finding Manville right away, as I think he is out of the city. However, I will find out where he is."

An hour passed in conversation without eliciting any thing new. Col. Tracy prepared to go out in search of George Manville. Claire was leaving the library when Col. Tracy requested that she should come to the library again at nine o'clock that evening, and he would report what success he had met with. Claire was strangely distracted all the afternoon, and little Nellie opened her brown eyes with astonishment, to find her poorly learned French lesson passed over without a reprimand, or even a gentle rebuke, from her teacher. While taking their music lesson, the same abstraction was visible. Her mind was in a chaos of hope and fear, doubt and perplexity.

Count Sayvord was lounging through the parlors with the air of man who is at a loss to know what disposal to make of *time*. He carelessly turned the leaves of elegantly bound volumes. Paintings and rare gems of art were looked at or handled with the same careless indifference. He tried to interest himself by looking at the beautiful grounds beyond the verandah, but some how his eyes would wander to where a graceful figure presided at the piano. When the lesson ended, the children pleaded for their accustomed song. Claire would gladly have excused herself, but Sayvord, who had joined the group, pleaded for just one song. Without further importuning, Claire sang an old ballad, which accorded well with her perturbed state of mind. Doubtless it touched an answering chord in the Count's heart, for he joined her in singing, and together their rich voices penetrated the hall, through which Isabelle was passing. She clenched her white hands until the pink, shell-like nails penetrated the tender flesh. The glittering black eyes spoke volumes of hate for the unconscious songstress. When the song ended, Claire sought her own room to think over the exciting events of the last twenty-four hours. In a little while Rose entered, holding a neat little volume of Tennyson's[1] poems very gingerly.

"Massa Count Sayvord say to present dis book, and hopes you will 'ruse it well."

A little exclamation of surprise escaped Claire as she took the book from the young girl. Rose left the room. As Claire mechani-

cally opened the little volume, a white note fluttered to the floor.
She picked it up. It ran as follows:

> MISS NEVILLE: —I hope you will pardon my seeming bold-
> ness. I have something of importance to communicate. This
> must be my excuse. Say that I can see you and when.
>
> > Respectfully,
> > SAYVORD.

Scarcely had the astonished girl finished the perusal of Sayvord's
strange note, when Rose reappeared, and placed the following note
in her hand:

> CLAIRE NEVILLE: —George Manville is dying. He wishes
> to see you. Come immediately in my carriage. Lose not a
> moment, or you may be too late.
>
> > DR. SINGLETON.

CHAPTER XX.   July 8, 1865

Death.

Dr. Singleton knew well how cautious Manville was, and how jeal-
ously he guarded his secret, and determined to use no false delicacy,
but abruptly to ask the question around which clustered such great
interests. The question was certainly abrupt, and some might feel

inclined to censure the doctor a little harshly for his injudicious haste but the doctor knew well the character he had to deal with.

Manville was startled by the question, so unlooked for, and which seemed indeed an echo of his own sad and troubled thoughts. And the emphatic avowal of the old gentleman, "I have found his daughter and wish to find means of communicating with him," startled him. He looked slightly disconcerted an instant, but resting his emaciated, trembling hand on Dr. Singleton's arm, said, in earnest and impressive tones, "I would give the slight hold I have upon life this instant, if I could see Richard Tracy, and just talk with him one hour. I have wronged him, how deeply God alone knows, and the thought is terrifying that I must die with this accursed memory of crime clinging to my mind. I have not the least idea where Richard is."

"I heard from a party of travelers a few years ago," said the doctor, "that he had been traveling restlessly about for years, and at last settled in the southern part of France, and was living the life of a recluse, seeking the society of none and visited by few."

"It seems hard," said Manville, "to die without being allowed to make even the slight restitution of which I am capable. I know that I cannot live much longer, for I am growing weaker with each passing breath, but I cannot die until I have atoned as far as lies in my power for the wrong done Richard Tracy. I could not live to see Richard touch our American shores again. Tell me, doctor, what shall I do?"

Dr. Singleton mused a moment, and said, "Write your confession, and I will promise to find Tracy, if he is living, and deliver it safely to him."

A spasm of pain distorted the pale face of Manville, as he expressively raised his mutilated right hand.

"I see," said the old man, "I was thoughtless, stupid, if you will, to forget that you had lost the use of that hand." The old gentleman looked thoughtful a moment, and then said, "Perhaps I could act as your amanuensis. If you wish, I will do so."

"I have been thinking of asking you to do so for some time," replied Manville, "but hesitated to request such a sacrifice of your time, which, I know, is so valuable."

"Oh, never mind the time!" said the doctor, good-naturedly. "Only tell me just what you want to say. Do not let false delicacy, nor any other motive, cause you to hesitate in making the last slight amendment for a life-time of wrong."

"Have no fear of that," said Manville. "Doctor, if you have writing materials at hand, we will begin *now*, for I feel that should we delay another day, it will be too late."

Dr. Singleton glanced at his patient, and felt his words to be true. Another day and it would be *too late*. Drawing a light stand to the side of the couch, and placing upon it the necessary articles, Dr. Singleton pronounced himself ready. Many times during the afternoon the old doctor was obliged to stop writing, to assist Elynthia in preparing stimulants and fanning Manville, who was sinking rapidly, while a mortal paleness overspread his countenance, and he spoke with difficulty. And at last the doctor had to bend his ear, to catch the faintly whispered words, but the dread confession once made, he seemed to breathe easier, and when he saw the manuscript made into a neat little package, and safely lodged in the doctor's capacious pocket, his dim eyes seemed to brighten for a moment, as he faintly whispered his thanks.

"Is there any thing more I can do for you?" asked Dr. Singleton.

"Nothing, Doctor."

"Is there any one whom you would like to see?"

"No one but Claire Tracy; were it possible for me to see her, and receive her forgiveness for the great wrong I have done her, I think I could die in peace."

"You shall see her," said the doctor, and he hurriedly penned a short note to Claire Neville, and dispatched his colored boy with his carriage to Col. Tracy's mansion.

In the mean time Manville was kept perfectly quiet, but his dim eyes were ever turned toward the door, and it was evident that he was intently listening for the arrival of the carriage. It came at last. There were footsteps in the narrow hall; the boy was not alone. A moment more and Claire Neville was ushered into the presence of the dying man. Dr. Singleton led her to the side of the couch, when Manville imploringly reached forth his left hand, and said, with difficulty:

"I am dying. I have wronged you deeply, but can you forgive me? Say that you can, and I die in peace."

"I forgive you," said the sweet voice of Claire, "as I hope my Father in heaven will forgive me."

"Tell Richard, when he returns, that my last breath was spent trying, and I hope not vainly, to undo some of the great wrong I have done him."

"I will do all you ask," said Claire. "But have you sought the forgiveness of One before whom you must stand to pass a solemn test. I can and do freely forgive you the wrong you have done me: only assure me that you are prepared to die, prepared to meet your God," and the pale, lovely creature, in her earnestness, had taken the hand of the dying man in both hers, and tears, large and pearly, fell upon Manville's face. He looked startled, and whispered, with thrilling earnestness:

"Pray for me, for I am *not* prepared. I cannot meet my God."

Claire knelt by the couch and fervently commended the soul which was fast approaching the gates of death to the mercy of the all wise Father. The last effort of Manville had been too much for his enfeebled state. A few crimson spots upon the white counterpane[1] told the startling truth.

"A hemorrhage," said the doctor softly, as he gently placed Manville in a more comfortable position. It was pitiful to witness the appealing look, in the glazing eyes, as they rested upon Dr. Singleton's face. Thus he died without one hope expressed in the great hereafter—died with the last rays of the setting sun, which fell lovingly upon the head of the kneeling girl. Dr. Singleton was deeply moved, and after regaining his composure, gently faced Claire and led her from the chamber of death. While placing her in the carriage, he said, taking her small hand in his, "Take courage, child, all will yet be well. The darkest hour precedes the dawn."

CHAPTER XXI.   July 15, 1865

Little Nellie's First Sorrow.

Heart-sick and weary, Claire sank back in the carriage, and was only roused from a painful reverie by their arrival at Col. Tracy's. Sayvord was sitting on the verandah, and regarded her earnestly as she walked slowly up the path with a sad, pale face, upon which remained the traces of recent tears. His presence reminded her of his requested interview.

As she was passing in the door little Nellie came bounding to her side, and said, while the beautiful brown eyes filled with tears,

"Mamma has been so sick, and she wanted to see you and you were gone, and papa was not here. Sister Belle and the servants did not know how to relieve her as you do, dear Miss Neville."

While Nellie was talking Claire was rapidly ascending the stairs. Divesting herself of bonnet and shawl, she hastened to Mrs. Tracy's room. Isabelle was sitting by the bed side, and several of the servants were in attendance. Isabelle's were the only eyes that did not smile a welcome to Claire as she entered the apartment.

Mrs. Tracy wearily opened her eyes, and, as her glance fell upon her young friend, an exclamation of glad surprise escaped her lips. But at last, noticing Claire's pale, care-worn face, she said, reproachfully,

"It is very selfish in me to wish for your attendance when you are ill yourself, but I have missed you sadly to-day. I have been suffering with a nervous headache, but I am better now, and you must retire early; for I see you are suffering as well as myself, and need rest. Isabelle can remain with me if I need any one."

Claire hastened to assure her she was not ill, and preferred to remain with her. And Isabelle, thinking of Sayvord, who was the sole occupant of the parlor, said,

"Yes, mamma, I think Miss Neville had better stay with you," and without waiting to hear her mother's remonstrance, swept from the room, and descended to the parlor, while Claire remained to soothe the weary invalid.

Sayvord had been anxiously waiting for a note or message from Claire, and now, as he heard light footsteps approaching, and the faint rustle of female garments, he hoped it might be her. His expressive face plainly betrayed his disappointment as the vision, not of the stately Claire, but the haughty Isabelle, dawned upon him. He rose with more haste than politeness, and coldly bowing to the discomfited young lady, left the room. Slowly the color faded from the beautiful face, and the black eyes were dilated with rage as she murmured the one expressive word, *infatuated*, and with that detested Yankee governess. A few moments she sat looking the very embodiment of anger and disappointment, then taking a seat at the piano, made it fairly tremble beneath her fingers, as she rattled through Polkas, Waltzes, Quadrilles, and Quick-steps,[1] in a manner that would have astonished our Claire; but it served somewhat in calming her excited feelings.

Claire possessed a sort of mesmeric influence over Mrs. Tracy. The soft touch of her velvet-like hands, the soothing tones of her sweet, musical voice, her swift, quiet movements as she flitted here and there through the apartment, were sleep-provoking in the extreme.

Nellie Tracy was soon calmly sleeping, and Claire sat by the window so quietly, that Lloyd, looking in his mother's room as he passed down to supper, did not notice the still figure sitting half-concealed by the light curtains, and wondered why her chair was vacant? Why, was it not enough to be absent from dinner? Where could she be? Sayvord and Col. Tracy, too, asked themselves the question: Where could she be? Little Nellie could scarcely eat for looking at the vacant chair by her side, and wondering what kept Miss Neville so long, thinking she must be very hungry. She did not eat any *dinner* either, thought the little one; she is almost starved I *know*. I'll go and ask mamma to let her come down to supper; and, intent upon her purpose, her kind, little heart filled with concern for the dear governess, whom her vivid imagination pictured as bordering on the state of starvation. Suddenly dropping her knife and fork, she slid from her chair, and ran hastily up stairs, never stopping until she reached her mother's room. Standing on tip-toe by the bed she could see that her mother was sleeping. Coming close to Claire's side, she peered earnestly into the sad, pale face, while the large eyes filled with tears, and a nervous twitching was visible about the corners of her rosy mouth.

"What is it, darling?" asked Claire, seeing the child was deeply agitated.

"You didn't eat any dinner, and now you are not coming down to supper," said she, and one after another, great tears rolled over her round cheeks and fell upon Claire's hand.

"Who thought there is one, at least, who thinks and cares for me," thought Claire, and she kissed the sweet one who pleaded so hard for her to only go to supper.

Claire would gladly have gone with the little girl, but she felt how utterly impossible it would be for her to eat one mouthful in her present state of mind, so she said:

"You are very thoughtful, Nellie, and I thank you very much for thinking of me. I do not wish any supper, and could not eat if I should go down, so you must excuse me to-night."

Nellie resolutely kept back her tears as she thought whatever ailed Miss Neville must be very *bad*. A person that hadn't eaten any *dinner* and yet didn't want any *supper* was a case beyond her childish comprehension. Without another word she turned, and went slowly back to the tea-room.

Sayvord had guessed her object in leaving the table, and looked disappointed when she returned alone. One glance at the vacant chair, and the little girl's fortitude gave way, and she sobbed aloud.

Col. Tracy looked surprised. "What is the matter with my little Nellie?" he asked.

"Why, she won't come," sobbed Nellie, unable to proceed for the moment.

"Who won't come?" asked her father, somewhat mystified as to her meaning

"Why, Miss Neville won't come down to supper, and she had no dinner. I know she is awful tired and hungry, for she is just as pale. Oh dear, oh dear," she said, pushing back her plate, "I don't want any supper either."

"I would not act so foolishly if a dozen Miss Nevilles would not come to their supper," said Belle, petulantly.

While Lloyd's sense of the ludicrous was so strong, that, utterly unable to suppress his risibles, his merry laugh echoed through the room, much to the distress of Nellie, who, fearing she had no sympathizers, utterly refused to be comforted, and, leaving the room, went out on the verandah, where she now sat looking very disconsolate.

Jim had been a quiet, though not an uninterested, spectator of the scene at the table, and the result was that he soon appeared by Nellie's side bearing a small tray, on which was a slice of delicately browned toast, a cup of fragrant tea, and several choice delicacies, very neatly arranged.

"Miss Nellie," said he, "let us take Miss Neville her supper."

Nellie had not thought of this, and the idea struck her as a good one and together they ascended the stairs followed by the earnest eyes of Count Sayvord.

CHAPTER XXII.   July 22, 1865

Across the Atlantic.

The scene changes. From the troubled household of the Tracy's, in the old Crescent City, we find ourselves transferred across the wide Atlantic, to the elegant country seat of Clayburn Sayvord, in the southern part of France, a few miles north of the beautiful city of Marseilles.

In a richly furnished apartment sit two gentlemen, quietly discussing the merits of a late breakfast. Let us closely observe them. The elder of the two, a little bright-eyed, sharp-nosed, old gentleman of nearly sixty, very diminutive in size, and faultless in style of dress, is Clayburn Sayvord. A pair of gold spectacles bestrode the sharp nose, through which the little gray eyes seemed to twinkle, as it were, with very kindness. His general appearance, from the hair of his carefully adjusted wig, to the tips of his elegant French boots, of the most delicate proportions, bespoke a good-natured, but *very particular* man—very precise in all his dealings with the world, shrewd and far-seeing. He was wont, when pleased, to rub his small, claw-like hands together much after the fashion of a pleased child. The character of the old gentleman will portray itself through the following chapters of our narrative.

The sad, thoughtful browed man who sat opposite, with large, melancholy black eyes, which mirrored forth a world of sadness from their quiet depths, is none other than our old friend Richard Tracy. But sorrow, not the flight of years, has furrowed the noble brow, and bowed the tall, lithe form; but it is our Richard still, with the old, sweet, winning smile. He comes to us again, after the lapse of many years, with heart and principles unchanged—the uncompromising advocate of equity and justice—the friend of the oppressed, and a bitter enemy of the accursed system of slavery, and its twin evil, *Caste*. Bitterly had he realized, and to its greatest extent, the misery, the horror, the degradation, and even *crime*, embodied in the sentence "The *curse of caste*." Would that the word could be blotted out at once and forever, from the memory of man.

Clayburn Sayvord was well acquainted with Richard's early history, and it was the topic of conversation this morning. Their conversation was brought to a close by the appearance of Pierre Dupont, the *valet de chambre*,[1] laden with dispatches, letters and papers, which he heaped upon a small silver tray, and placed by M. Sayvord's side, who, rubbing his hands gleefully said:

"Really, this looks like business."

He passed the papers to Richard who had received no letters by this mail, settled himself more comfortably in his chair, and prepared to read the letters from his numerous correspondents. The dispatches were read and carefully laid aside. Letter after letter was perused, when he took up rather a bulky letter, bearing the New Orleans post-mark.

"A letter from your old home," he said, looking at Richard. "From the Count," he continued, as he carefully polished the glass, and readjusted the gold spectacles. Then, carefully re-settling himself in his chair, (by the way, M. Sayvord did every thing *carefully*) the better to digest the contents of the letter, which certainly was long, and promised to be interesting. After reading a little while, Monsieur became very red in the face, and altogether quite fidgety, casting frequent and expressive glances at Richard, who was deeply absorbed in a speech of Lord Brougham's,[2] but was finally attracted by Monsieur's frequent exclamations, such as, "O!" "Wonderful!" and so on, to the end of the chapter of interjections. He could not suppress a smile as M. Clayburn Sayvord, laying down the letter, polished his glasses again, and this time most carefully adjusted them to prepare to read it the second time, after which he turned to Richard abruptly, and said, with startling distinctness:

"Tracy, did it never occur to you that there may have been some mistake in the reported death of your child? Have you proof that the child died? Do you know where it was buried? What do you know, or do you know any thing about the matter?" asked the excited little man (while the glasses were in imminent danger of another removal).

Richard's heart throbbed painfully, as he thought what these strange questions might presage. He hardly dared allow himself to think. Had he not trusted too implicitly in the honor of others?

"I have no proof but Manville's word. He wrote that my infant daughter died immediately after birth, and was entombed with its mother. I visited Lina's grave before leaving the United States."

"But where was Juno, the black nurse?" asked Monsieur. "Could she not have told better than any one else?"

"Juno was devoted to my frail young wife, and I never could quite understand why she went away without waiting to see me. She must have known that I would come. I gave Manville permission to do with every thing as he deemed best. The cottage and furniture became the home and property of Mr. Villars. Juno had moved away, but where, they (the Villars) could not tell. But why this strange questioning? What does it portend?"

"Read the Count's letter," was Monsieur's only reply, as he passed the letter to Richard.

Count Sayvord, in his letter, had given a most minute description of Claire Neville, her advent in the Tracy family, her striking resemblance to the family, the mystified air of Colonel Tracy and Lloyd, the astonishment of the negroes, the hatred of the haughty Isabelle toward the beautiful Yankee governess, were all faithfully drawn. One paragraph read as follows:

> There is a sad story connected with this family. Uncle, you remember Richard Tracy, the sad browed man who was visiting you at the country seat, some years ago? Well, that same Richard is Col. Tracy's oldest son. His marriage displeased his father, though for what reason I have yet to learn, but it is believed by every one that Claire is the offspring of that marriage, and the granddaughter of Col. Tracy. Of course, there is no proof of such being the true state of affairs, but I with all others, believe

it to be the true version of the case. I have determined to unravel the mystery, let it be what it will. If Richard Tracy is with
you, or you know where he is, tell him of Claire Neville, and
all I have written to you of the family. Learn what you can of
his life history, and transmit the same to me without delay. I
will keep you well informed as to my success.

Your nephew,
SAYVORD.

CHAPTER XXIII.   July 29, 1865

This Side of the Atlantic.

Monsieur Sayvord finished the reading of his letters, and glanced
anxiously at Richard, who was sitting motionless, absorbed in
thought, with the open letter before him. Monsieur wondered what
he could be thinking of, that he did not speak.

Yes, Richard was thinking. Far back through the hazy vistas of the
past, came sweet and bitter memories, hand in hand. Again he stood
with his lovely betrothed upon the deck of the noble Alhambra,—
again he pressed to his heart the trembling form of his blushing
bride, and imprinted the first husband's kiss upon her pure brow.
Again he and his gentle Lina were the happy inmates of Rose Cottage, while Juno, sitting 'neath the shade of the lofty tamaracks,
forced a pleasing picture in the back-ground. Again he was parting with—was looking for the *last* time upon the sweet, pale face

shadowed by undefined sorrow. The journey south; the interview with his angry father; the long, weary days when his spirits feebly fluctuated between life and death; his partial recovery; the weary, weary, waiting for the letter which would never come again; Manville's visit to Rose Cottage; the letter; the death of his wife and child; the darker days which followed, when his unceasing prayer had been that he too, might die,—might sleep the long, dreamless sleep, which knows no waking here on earth; that last visit to his young wife's grave; his departure from the United States, and the long years of lonely wandering, of aimless existence, that followed. All passed, in rapid review before his mind's eye.

Now came this letter from Count Sayvord, so strange as to appear impossible, that this young girl, whom the Count speaks of as being strangely beautiful and accomplished, could be his child. No. It could not be.

Had not Manville written that the child had died, and was buried with its young mother? Had he not visited their lone grave on the hillside, where the twinkling stars kept nightly vigil, and the night-winds sighed a requiem for the loved and early lost. No, it could not be. But all the while his heart thrilled strangely. And the name of Claire Neville, where had he heard it before? It sounded strangely familiar. A moment of intense thought, and he had solved the mystery surrounding the name of Claire Neville. He had often heard Lina speak of a dear school-friend, bearing that name. This knowledge suggested another thought, and a tiny spark of hope burned in his heart. A hope that *this* Claire, so far away, between himself and whom rolled the waters of the wide Atlantic, might prove to be his own dear child.

So he thought on, unconscious of Monsieur, who sat opposite, nearly convulsed with excitement and curiosity suppressed, trying to school his patience until Richard should speak. But time sped on; an hour had passed, yet Richard moved not, spoke not,—only hoped and dreamed on, with the open letter before him. Monsieur looked uneasily at Richard, fidgeted about in his chair, and finally got up and put his letters and papers away, hoping thus to attract the attention of his friend, but in vain. What should he do to arouse him? The expediency of the letter being answered immediately presented itself. Hastily crossing the room, he laid his hand upon Richard's shoulder, and said, very emphatically:

"Tracy, this letter must be answered this hour, in order to catch the first mail, which leaves at 4 p.m. It is now half past twelve. So you see, man, it behooves us to be moving."

This had the desired effect. Richard was awake, and ready to begin the work before him. Monsieur rang the bell, ordered the breakfast dishes removed, and writing materials placed in their stead. For a long while no sound was heard save that caused by rapidly moving pens, over vast sheets of snowy paper, and at precisely five minutes of four o'clock, two bulky letters were sealed and directed, and Pierre Dupont summoned to mail them.

Richard had faithfully narrated every incident connected with his married life, that could serve in any way to throw light upon the real parentage of the young girl, with the urgent request that Count Sayvord would learn all facts relating to the childhood of Claire Neville, and compare them with his letters, and, knowing his anxiety, to write to him at length.

Upon the reception of these letters, Count Sayvord felt more confident than ever that Claire was Richard Tracy's daughter, and upon the strength of these letters he resolved to ask her confidence, and then tell her all he had learned.

With this object in view, he penned a hasty note requesting an interview, and dispatched it by Rose in a small volume of Tennyson's poems, and waited impatiently for a reply. He saw Claire depart a few minutes afterwards, attended only by a young negro boy. He noted the exceeding paleness of her face, and wondered what was the meaning of so strange a proceeding. He seated himself upon the verandah to await her return.

The Count was beginning to grow restless, and glanced frequently up and down the long street, when the carriage rolled into view. He watched her with a tender light in his large blue eyes, as she stepped slowly and wearily up the long walk. Her pale face was worn and weary. He expected, at least, to see her at tea time, but she did not appear. He sympathized heartily in little Nellie's sorrow. He knew Claire was suffering, and he determined to reward Jim handsomely for his thoughtfulness of the governess' welfare.

Jim and Nellie entered the room very quietly, so as not to wake Mrs. Tracy. Nellie hastily transferred the books and ornaments from a small stand to a chair, placed the stand by Claire's side, upon which Jim placed the silver tray with a well-pleased air.

"Now, Miss Neville, you must drink some of this tea. 'Tis the very best, and Aunt Hopsy says it will do you as much good as the 'tents of a hull potecary[1] shop."

Claire smiled faintly, and Nellie said, coaxingly:

"Please, Miss Neville, eat just a little supper. If you don't, I'll tell papa to send for Doctor Thorne, and then you will wish you had taken my advice, if I am a little girl."

Nellie, with an assumption of great dignity, motioned Jim to follow her, and softly closing the door, they went down stairs.

Claire did not offer to taste the contents of the little tray, but pressing her fingers to her aching brow, longed for the hour of nine, when she was to meet Col. Tracy. Then she would be at liberty to retire. She turned to look at the little clock on the mantle, but she could not distinguish the figures. The little time-piece usually so staid and orderly, was actually executing a pirouette,[2] after the most approved fashion. Vases and perfumery bottles, and various little mantle and table ornaments, seemed to be infected with the same spirit, and were merrily

"Tripping the light fantastic-toe"[3]

The chairs were very neighborly, and were rapidly changing position. The pictures on the wall expressed their approbation of the proceedings by swinging lazily back and forth.

"I must be going crazy," murmured Claire, tightly pressing her burning brow. Then bursting into a wild, hysterical laugh, she fell heavily to the floor.

That laugh, so wild and ringing, followed by the heavy fall, awoke Mrs. Tracy, who, in her extreme fright, alternately screamed and pulled the bell-cord.

CHAPTER XXIV.   August 5, 1865

Poor Claire.

The frantic cries of Mrs. Tracy, together with the violent ringing of the bell in the servant's hall, brought the entire household to her assistance. Lloyd was first to enter the apartment. He advanced towards his mother, while surprise and alarm were plainly portrayed upon his fine face. Mrs. Tracy motioned him back, and pointed to the prostrate form of Claire. An exclamation of mingled astonishment and regret escaped his lips, and he gently raised the inanimate form to the sofa, as Col. Tracy, Sayvord, and Isabelle entered, followed by a troop of frightened negroes, whose dusky faces thronged every available door and window. A hurried consultation was held, and Jim was sent in haste to summon Dr. Thorne, the family physician.

Jim made all possible speed and soon arrived at the residence of Dr. Thorne, which worthy gentleman he found busily discussing the chemical qualities of a new medicine, with none other than our friend, Dr. Singleton.

Jim entered the doctor's study without ceremony. He was quite a favorite with the gentleman, and proceeded, while the doctor was getting ready, to give a short version of the case: how Miss Neville had gone away in a strange carriage, and returned, looking so pale, and just as if she had been crying; how she had refused to come down to supper, and he and Miss Nellie had taken up her tea on the little tray, and left her sitting by the window, looking awful pale; how they had just got down stairs when the bell rang violently, and terrible screams were heard coming from Mrs. Tracy's room; how Col. Tracy and every body ran up stairs, and found Massa Lloyd lifting the governess to the sofa.

"Then I was sent for you," said Jim, ending with a bow, and stood, hat in hand, waiting Dr. Thorne's orders.

The doctor turned to his friend with the intention of apologizing for his hurried departure, when Dr. Singleton precluded the necessity of so doing, by saying,

"Thorne, I am greatly interested in this young lady; besides, I have an *object* in wishing to be introduced to the Tracy family, and if you have no objection, I will accompany you."

"Very well, you are quite welcome to go, if it be your desire," replied Thorne, wondering much, on their way to the carriage, what could be Singleton's object in wishing so particularly, to become acquainted with the Tracy's, but that he had an object, he did not doubt, for Dr. Singleton was never guilty of jesting.

Arriving at Col. Tracy's, the doctors were shown to Mrs. Tracy's room, and after applying the proper restoratives, it was long ere Claire exhibited signs of returning life. At last, after moving slightly, she slowly opened her large black eyes, and gazed from one to the other of the anxious faces above her, with a bright but meaningless glance. Alas! the light of reason had fled those beautiful orbs. Searchingly the bright eyes seemed to rest upon each face. Isabelle, who had been standing somewhat in the shadow, now stepped directly under the blazing chandelier. When Claire's gaze fell upon her, she uttered a piercing shriek, clasping her hands convulsively over her eyes, as if to shut out some hateful vision.

"Mercy, oh, have mercy!" she shrieked. "Those eyes are burning through my brain. Save me, oh, save me! She will kill me!"

The doctors exchanged glances of surprise, while Isabelle, secretly determining to annoy her as much as possible, turned away with a mocking smile.

Dr. Singleton placed his hand on Claire's brow, much after the fashion he used to do with Richard, and was surprised at the likeness existing between the two. Claire's illness was pronounced brain fever.[1]

"Brought on," added Dr. Singleton, "by unusual excitement, and excessive strain on the mental faculties."

Little Nellie was almost heart-broken, and utterly refused to be comforted. Col. Tracy sought to lead the child from the room, but she utterly refused to go unless first allowed to kiss Miss Neville. Her father lifted her up to kiss the pale, sweet face. Nellie pressed her little, chubby hands to both Claire's cheeks, and kissed her crimson lips repeatedly, while burning tears rolled over her cheeks.

"I will go now, Papa," she said, with a choking voice, and was carried, sobbing, from the room. Laura, less demonstrative than Nellie, passed quietly from the sick room, and sought the deserted parlor, where, unobserved, she could quietly indulge her grief. Claire was a favorite with all the negroes, and the house that night looked gloomy with their sad, dusky faces.

Claire was delirious all night. Sometimes she raved of great, burning, black eyes. Sometimes of Juno, and her northern home. Sometimes she called plaintively for Miss Elwood; then she would hold long talks with her dear friend, Ella Summers. Again she would ask, in ringing tones:

"Who am I? Oh, some one tell me! This suspense will kill me. If Richard *is* my father, why don't he come? Oh, George Manville, why did you rob me of a father's love? It was cruel."

Thus it was for days. No dawning of returned reason for the suffering girl. No dawn of hope for the anxious physicians. It seemed almost in vain that the queenly little head was shorn of its wealth of purple black hair, but Dr. Singleton said that was their last hope. So the barber was called in, and the sharp, glittering, ruthless shears soon severed the heavy mass, which lay, bright and shining, upon the snowy counterpane. Almost in vain it seemed, that every care was bestowed, that every remedy was applied. Vain it seemed, were the prayers of Mrs. Tracy, always joined by dear little Nellie, whose solemn and fervently uttered prayer, "*Please God, do make dear Miss Neville well*," was affecting to hear. Mrs. Tracy loved and wept over her darling child.

Poor Claire had a warm place in many hearts. And now the old house, void of her sweet smiles and songs, was *too* lonely. Isabelle wondered if Claire would get well, and every time her glance fell upon that well-shaped head, shorn of its crowning glory, a triumphant smile curled her scornful lips. Isabelle was compelled to visit the room when Claire was sleeping, for during her wakeful hours, Isabelle's presence in the room rendered her almost unmanageable. She imagined Isabelle some destroying spirit from whose baleful influence there was no escape. Thus we leave our Claire for the present, to look after old Juno, the faithful friend and nurse.

CHAPTER XXV.   August 12, 1865

Juno.

Just after you turn the bend in the long, dusty road leading many miles from the thriving town of L—, you can espy through a wilderness of shrubbery, a neat little cottage, almost embowered in green trees and trailing vines. The cottage presents such a pleasing exterior, that we will extend our ramble, and learn something of its inmates. As we pass through the gate and up the neatly arranged walk, our eyes are almost blinded by coming in contact with a pyramid of shining milk pans, which reflect the rays of the sun. Passing the moss-grown well, whose waters look cool and sparkling, we are constrained to quaff a draught from the gourd, hanging at its side. Entering the cozy kitchen, whose snowy chairs, table and floor, with rows of shining tins, and polished cooking stove are forcibly suggestive of neatness and comfort. Baskets filled with newly washed muslins, looking very much like great drifts of snow, were standing waiting the deft hands of the mistress of the cottage, who, standing before one of the snowy tables, is deep in the mysteries of sprinkling.

The countenance, pleasing and familiar, is that of Juno, slightly changed by the lapse of years, only a little more corpulent. We will here state for the satisfaction of the reader, that soon after Claire had entered L— Seminary, Juno, in consideration of her extreme loneliness, had taken to herself a husband. Martin Ray was a worthy, industrious man, with an unlimited confidence in his wife's opinion. They lived quietly and happily together.

On this afternoon, as Juno carefully dampens and rolls the clothes into compact rolls, she thoughtfully soliloquizes:

"No use trying to deceive Juno! I know Claire is in trouble. Something's happened, or what is the meaning of all these strange dreams. Martin said that when I dreamed that Squire Farley's barn burned, it signified hasty news. Martin's going to L— to-morrow. He must go and see Miss Ellwood and ask about the child. It seems an awful while since I heard from Claire, an' this poor old heart is longing for the precious lamb. After all, perhaps I was wrong not to tell Claire who her father was. If I had, she never would have gone to be governess in old Col. Tracy's family. But I always thought it best that Claire should never know she was tainted with black blood. But I must say, this child don't see the difference,—don't see why black blood ain't just as good as white any day! (Unsophisticated Juno, others have asked the same question, without receiving a satisfactory answer). But I always thought Claire would hate me if I told her about it. So I put it off again and again. But it's got to come out some time, and might as well have been first as last. But it is too late now. I didn't tell her before, and somehow I feel that Master Richard *will come*, and tell it all himself. And I believe he will," she said, as she finished laying the white shirts, compactly rolled, into the basket, just as Martin entered, with two brimming pails of milk.

"We must have a good, long talk this evening," she said, as she proceeded to strain the milk into four shining milk pans.

After putting it carefully away in the cool spring-house,[1] she prepared their evening meal, and all the evening chores completed, Martin and Juno repaired to the pleasant, vine-wreathed porch, to have the promised talk. It was late ere they retired, and after Martin had interpreted Juno's dreams for the fiftieth time, perhaps, it was decided that when Martin went to L— on the following day, he should go and see Miss Ellwood and ask her all about Claire.

———

It was late in the afternoon, and piles of spotless shirts, with bosoms glossy and stiff, displayed the house-wife's industry. Juno walked frequently to the door, and shading her eyes from the rays of the setting sun, gazed wistfully down the long, dusty road, and failing to see Martin, returned to her ironing table.

At last she recognized Bobby, Martin's horse, in the distance. She waited their nearer approach, and finding that Martin was not alone, hastened to throw open the pretty little parlor.

"Miss Ellwood, as I live!" exclaimed Juno, delightedly, as she ushered the good lady into the cool and inviting room, and placed the rocking chair for her greater comfort, and impatiently waited to hear what she was indebted for the honor of the visit. Miss Ellwood looked very grave, as she gently said:

"Juno, I am very sorry to be the bearer of bad news."

Juno looked a little frightened, as the lady proceeded to tell how she had received a letter from Col. Tracy, written in great haste, stating that Claire was very ill, perhaps would never recover, and requesting that Miss Ellwood would find Claire's old nurse, and find out who Claire's parents really were, and also obtain any little keep-sake or memento that had belonged to either of the parents.

"It is of the utmost importance that we have this proof, and hope you will lose no time in seeking out the black nurse, and transmitting to me the knowledge obtained," wrote Col. Tracy, in conclusion.

"Now, Juno," said Miss Ellwood, addressing the weeping woman, "you must not cry, but sit down here, by my side, and tell me all you know of Claire's father and mother."

Taking out her writing materials, which she had brought with her, she proceeded to narrate the facts as Juno stated them. After finishing the letter, Miss Ellwood asked if there were any letters that had passed between Richard and Lina, or any thing that would assist in unraveling the mystery surrounding her dear young friend.

Juno produced the rosewood box. Miss Ellwood looked over the letters and little ornaments, and finding the certificate of the marriage of Richard and Lina, she proceeded to make them into a package to forward by the next mail to Col. Tracy. After thanking Juno, and bidding her be of good cheer, Miss Ellwood departed.

But we must leave Juno in her quiet cottage home, and hie[2] again to bonny France, and learn what has transpired in our absence.

CHAPTER XXVI.   August 19, 1865

Richard counted the days and hours it would take his letter to reach the United States, then how long it would take it to reach New Orleans. But, count as he would, it seemed almost an age until he could receive an answer, even if the Count replied immediately.

Hours were spent in dreaming over the Claire so far away. Many times he sketched her face, as he imagined it must be beautiful and pale, with hair and eyes intensely black. He would gaze long and lovingly upon the beautiful shadows he created, and hoped the original of the sweet vision might prove to be his child and Lina's. It would be a happiness that language would prove inadequate to express; it would compensate him in a degree for long years of suffering. But then—and the thought came sadly and bitterly—the *curse* would be upon her, too. That thought was enough to drive all pleasing anticipations far from him, and introduce perplexing and harrowing meditations. So he allowed himself to brood over the matter, and grow more unhappy and very taciturn in consequence thereof.

Mons. Sayvord was wild with excitement and as impatient as his friend to hear from the Western world. He passed the most of his leisure time in trying to conjecture how the affair would end, and if Claire would really prove to be Richard's daughter. Twenty times a day he would startle his friend in the midst of a painful reverie by asking some strange question, which had presented itself to his fertile brain, and as many times declaring his intention of taking a journey to New Orleans himself. "I am an old man, I know," he would add, "but I know I could stand it. Will you go, Richard?" But the latter shrank from the thought of visiting his old home. He had suffered so much, so bitterly, that he deemed the ordeal more than he could bear.

"Pshaw, Tracy, be a man! Such thoughts are unworthy of you! Make up your mind to go and investigate this matter for yourself. Say that you will go, and I will accompany you to the 'land of the free and the home of the brave.'"

They finally concluded to await another letter from the Count. Then, if it should seem necessary, they would start immediately.

So they waited impatiently through the long weeks that followed
ere the letter came. It came at last—but not so full of hope as they
could have desired. Its burden was:

> Claire Neville, we fear, is dying; but I feel more convinced
> than ever that she *is* Richard Tracy's child. We have quite an
> eccentric character here, a Dr. Singleton, who seems singu-
> larly interested in the young governess. I sometimes think he
> knows something of her parents, and I have determined to
> ask him on the first opportunity that presents itself. He is an
> intimate friend of Dr. Thorne, the family physician—and if
> Claire Neville ever recovers, it will be owing to the skill and
> untiring zeal of Dr. Singleton, who says he hopes, through
> God, to bring her back to health. You will hear from me again
> soon. I will address my next to Richard. I expect to have some-
> thing of importance to write him.

After concluding the letter, Sayvord said, "Well, Richard, what
do you say now—will you go to America nor not?"

Richard hesitated awhile, but finally reluctantly consented to
go; but many times during their preparation for departure, he re-
pented of his weakness in promising Mons. Sayvord to take this
voyage, and would fain have given it up. But Monsieur, full of life
and spirits, was quite captivated with the idea of going to America.
"Oh, I know I shall stand the journey," he would say to his friend;
"may be a little sea-sick crossing the Atlantic, but I cannot expect
any thing else!"

Whenever Richard expressed his unwillingness to go, Monsieur
rallied him unmercifully upon his lack of fortitude and strength of
resolution; but at last all preparations were completed, and the journey to Havre[1] accomplished, without any thing occurring to mar
Monsieur's felicity and good spirits. His unfailing good humor was
contagious, and Richard, becoming infected with it, grew cheerful

and hopeful, and it was decided that before they proceeded to New Orleans, they should visit Richard's old home, Rose Cottage. Monsieur was terribly sea-sick while crossing the Atlantic, but the little old gentleman bore it bravely, never once giving up the belief that he could and would stand it. Arriving in Boston, they remained a few days to get rested and enable Monsieur to see the lions.[2] Then they entered Connecticut, and upon reaching the thriving manufacturing town of Danbury,[3] found no longer the old Ruthford stage, which was now classed among the things that were, and of which, only the memory remained. The cars now passed through the little village, towards which Richard was wending his way. While standing upon the platform at the neat little depot waiting for the train, which was somewhat late, Richard was accosted by an old lady, whose corpulency of proportion amused him somewhat, but whose gentle becoming smile prepossessed him in her behalf.

"Will you please see that I get safely on board the cars—for I never was on them, and I feel a little timid."

Richard would do this, of course; and, upon asking her destination, was surprised to find it the same as his own. And when at last they were comfortably rested in the cars, Richard began conversing with the old lady, who was none other than Mrs. Butterworth, the nurse, looking scarcely a day older than when we saw her last at Rose Cottage.

Mrs. Butterworth was very communicative, and talked of the inhabitants of Ruthford and surrounding villages for twenty-five years back. "Who knows," thought Richard, "but this very pleasant old lady may know something of Rose Cottage and its inmates!" He resolved to ask her. In reply to his question, the old lady said:

"I don't know the family that lives in the Cottage now; for it is many years since I was there. Let me see," she added, thoughtfully, "I guess it is about eighteen years this very fall since I went to nurse Mrs. Tracy, a young, delicate creature, who died in that Cottage, leaving a beautiful infant daughter to the care of an old colored nurse. If I should live to be a much older woman than I am, I never could forget that young, dying wife's prayer for her absent husband."

CHAPTER XXVII.   August 26, 1865

Mrs. Butterworth's Revelation.

"Her last words were, when asked if she had no word to leave for her husband, for she avoided speaking of him, 'Tell him I loved and—,' but the sentence was never finished. Poor, young thing! It was well she died as soon as she did," continued the matter-of-fact Mrs. Butterworth, who had thus far failed to notice the extreme agitation of her questioners, "for her husband was a villain, and she escaped a great many trials, by passing from the earth thus early."

Richard was deeply agitated, and motioning Monsieur Sayvord to proceed with questioning their fellow-traveler, he prepared to await further developments. Monsieur Sayvord proceeded to question the old lady with his usual abruptness.

"So the child *did not* die, you say?"

"No, sir; it lived, and was as fine and healthy a child as you could wish to see."

"What was the colored nurse's name?"

"Juno Hays."

"And what induced you to think that Mrs. Tracy's husband was a villain?"

"Why," replied the old lady, her round, honest eyes flashing with indignation, "if he had been a good and honorable man, he would have written to his poor little heart-broken wife, as a husband ought. He would never have gone to Europe without her knowledge, leaving her among strangers to die alone. May God forgive the wicked man, wherever he may be!"

"How do you know he went to Europe? And what became of the child and nurse?"

Mrs. Butterworth then related the particulars of Manville's visit, the sale of Rose Cottage, and subsequent removal of Juno and baby Claire to the eastern part of the State. That was all she knew, and since that time she had lost all trace of them.

"But," suggested Mrs. Butterworth, seeing how deeply interested the gentlemen were, "I think Dr. Murdoch could tell you more concerning them. Maybe you're a relation?" she said inquiringly.

Without answering her question directly, Monsieur Sayvord replied:

"We are very much interested in any thing that relates to Mrs. Tracy, and thank you for the information you have given. And I wish to disabuse your mind of false opinions concerning Richard Tracy. I know him well. He is a true and noble man, and mourns yet the early death of his young and gentle wife, who, with himself, was the victim of that designing villain, Manville. Through his representations, Richard has believed, until very recently, that the child had died immediately after birth, and was buried with its mother."

Mrs. Butterworth was very much astonished at this view of the case, but readily transferred her indignation from Richard to Manville. And our friend possessed *her* sympathy as he has always had ours.

Arriving at the end of their journey, they parted company with the old nurse, and repaired to the best hotel the village afforded. After Richard had partially regained his composure, and they had partaken of a genuine New England dinner, they started in quest of Dr. Murdoch, the old village physician, whose professional business was now carried on by Dr. Murdoch, Jr. The old gentleman was pleased with their visit, and cheerfully related what he knew of the inmates of Rose Cottage. It wrung Richard's heart to hear him talk so touchingly about Lina.

"Mr. Villars owns the cottage now. He bought it, furniture and all, when that dashing young Southerner came and took away Juno and the little baby, who was fast becoming a great favorite with me. I suppose she is a young lady now," said the old doctor, thoughtfully. "Ah, me! how time flies. Why, it is eighteen years ago, and I was an old man *then*."

"Do you know to what town or village they moved?"

"Somewhere in the vicinity of the town of L—, but that you know, was so long ago, they may have moved again."

Thus learning all they could, they took leave of Dr. Murdoch, and returned to the hotel, when they determined, much to the discomfiture of the landlord, who did not like the idea of losing two such distinguished guests, to take the night express for Danbury, and so be enabled to take the first eastern train the following day. It was their intention to seek out Juno before starting for New Orleans. They knew Claire was ill,—perhaps dying, but Richard felt that he *must* see Juno first. And impatient as was Monsieur Sayvord, he thought it best to go to L— and make inquiry concerning the old nurse.

Taking the night express they arrived at Danbury at 4 a.m., and taking the train for the east at 11 a.m., they reached L— at seven o'clock on the morning of the following day. After a fresh toilet, and a hasty breakfast, they started out upon their tour of inquiry. For a long time they could learn nothing. It was very evident Juno did not live in L—.

"She may be living in the country, some where," suggested Monsieur, as he noticed his friend's despairing look. "Here comes a nice looking colored man, let us ask him."

This colored man proved to be none other than Thomas, Miss Ellwood's hired man, who built fires, and did chores about the Seminary. In answer to their inquiry, Thomas replied:

"Yes, sir; there is such a woman living a few miles from this place. I do not know much about her myself, but the lady I live with can tell you, for she often comes to the Seminary, to see Miss Ellwood, and before Miss Claire left school, Juno used to visit her sometimes."

"Well, my man, I think we have been very fortunate in meeting you, and you will further oblige us by leading the way to the Seminary."

Miss Ellwood was quite astonished when she learned that one of her unexpected guests was the son of Col. Tracy, and more astonished when he declared himself to be the father of her favorite pupil, Claire Neville. She told him how Manville had placed Claire in the Seminary, six years before with the understanding that she (Miss Ellwood) was to spare neither pains nor expense upon the child's education. The bills were always regularly paid, one year in advance. She told Richard much of Claire's disposition and habits, and related many little incidents of her school life.

Thomas had returned from the post-office in the mean time, bringing various letters for Miss Ellwood, one of which was from Col. Tracy, acknowledging the receipt of her package. Richard waited with ill-concealed impatience, until she had finished reading the somewhat lengthy epistle. Miss Ellwood turned to him with a smile when she had finished the letter and said, gently—

CHAPTER XXVIII.   September 2, 1865

Further Developments.

"'Claire is better,' Col. Tracy writes. 'We dare to indulge the hope that she will again be restored to perfect health. The certificate and letters prove beyond the least semblance of a doubt that Claire Neville is our grand-daughter—the offspring of my son's unfortunate union. We can, of course, say nothing of this to Claire for a long time to come. But I frequently ask myself, 'Where is my son, whom I have made an exile from his native land?' You, of course, know nothing of *him*. But if, by any strange or unexpected combination of circumstances, you should learn any thing concerning him, lose no time in transmitting the knowledge to me.'"

A sigh of relief escaped Richard, as Miss Elwood ceased speaking. He would yet press his darling child to his heart, which was already overflowing with paternal love. And his father, it was evident, had not quite forgotten.

It was decided that Mons. Sayvord and Richard should remain the guests of Miss Elwood until the following day, when, in company with their kind hostess, they would pay a visit to old Juno.

"Martin, I had a strange dream, last night, and shall hear good news ere the day closes," said Juno, cheerfully.

Martin looked up, with a gratified smile. He was gladdened by any thing that betokened a return of Juno's wonted[1] spirits; for ever since she learned of Claire's illness, she had been sad and silent, frequently indulging in long crying spells.

Martin had often reasoned with her, and persuaded her to be more hopeful, but all to no purpose, for Juno persistently refused to be comforted. But on this glorious morning Juno seemed more like her former self. And at noon, when Martin returned to dinner, he found Juno singing, and seemingly somewhat excited. Every window was hoisted, every door was at its widest extension, while carpets and furniture underwent a thorough sweeping and dusting. Martin looked on in perfect astonishment, as his wife hurriedly put the various articles in their proper places. "Why, Juno, what do you mean?" he found time and breath to ask, as Juno peremptorily ordered him to kill two of the spring pullets.[2]

"Well," said she, in reply, "the truth is, I expect company."

"*Who*?" queried Martin, eagerly.

"Oh, I don't know who—but the rooster crowed before the door three times this morning; so I know somebody's coming; and I want to be prepared, that's all."

After they were seated at the table, Juno sat for some minutes looking thoughtfully into her tea-cup, and then said, in low and impressive tones:

"Martin, I tell you, *Master Richard is coming*. I know it. I feel it. He may not come to-day, nor yet to-morrow, but *he is coming*, and that very soon, too."

Martin thought it was very likely that Richard would come. If his wife had said, "Martin, the moon will fall to-morrow night," he would have believed it quite possible. However, the meal dispatched and the two spring pullets killed, Martin returned to his work in the south meadow, while Juno, upon the strength of her dreams and the crowing chanticleer, continued her busy preparation. She frequently sought the door, and strained her eyes far down the dusty road, but failing to discern any one in the distance, returned to her work. But ere long her attentive ear caught the sound of wheels. She ran to the door just in time to see Miss Elwood coming up the neatly bordered walks, accompanied by two gentlemen. Juno bent one piercing glance upon the taller of the two gentlemen, and sank in a chair, exclaiming in an excited voice, "God be praised! It is Master Richard!"

And when the two entered the little parlor, and Richard shook her warmly by the hand, saying, "My dear old friend, I am rejoiced to see you!" Juno could only sob aloud and fervently ejaculate: "Thank the Lord! Thank the Lord!"

It was some time before she was composed enough to relate to Richard the closing scenes in his young wife's life. The entire party was more or less affected as Juno, in simple but eloquent words, repeated Lina's trials—how the young wife's cheek grew pale and her step feeble as she waited with breaking heart for the letter that would never come; how she turned away with a look of hopeless despair in her beautiful eyes; and how, at last, a letter came, and proved fatal in its cruel mission; a night of sorrow, and the cloudless morning dawned upon a beautiful new-born babe, and the lifeless form of the young mother; how she and the old nurse, Mrs. Butterworth, had watched with pride and wonder over baby Claire until Manville came, telling her that Richard was in Europe, and advising the sale of Rose Cottage, and her removal to the eastern part of the State.

Richard grew more astonished and indignant as each successive revelation served to disclose more fully the duplicity of Manville. When Juno concluded her narrative, he related all that had taken place after he bade them farewell at the door of Rose Cottage, until he stood with gentle Addie Villiers by his young wife's grave. When he had finished, Juno said, "I never believed the wrong was in *you*, Master Richard. I always thought and said you would come. I never told Claire who her father was, because I wanted her to respect you; but, thank God, it will all be made right."

A long time they remained talking over the past. Martin returned from the field and was met at the door by the triumphant Juno, who exclaimed:

"Martin, Martin, he has come! Master Richard is here!"

Martin could only gaze upon his wife as one in a dream. He listened incredulously as she excitedly repeated, "Master Richard has come!" and seriously began to think his better-half was not quite right. But his doubts were dispelled by the pleasant voice of Miss Elwood:

"Come in, Martin, and see Mr. Tracy."

Martin received an introduction awkwardly enough, and regarded Richard as an object of great interest and worthy of his undivided attention.

After doing justice to Juno's spring-pullets, the company took their leave in order to secure a good night's rest ere they started on their long journey south. They bid Juno and Martin good-by with much regret, and proceeded on their way with hopeful hearts; and, for once in his life, perhaps, Mons. Sayvord was silent. The travelers left L— by an early train on the following morning. But, leaving them to pursue their journey alone, we will precede them to New Orleans.

CHAPTER XXIX.   September 9, 1865

Convalescent.

Claire was convalescent, and an air of cheerfulness reigned throughout the household of the Tracys. Mrs. Tracy spent the most of her time by the couch upon which the invalid reclined—she whose cheeks and short raven locks formed a beautiful contrast with the crimson pillows. Every one, from the stern old Colonel down to the youngest urchin about the establishment, seemed desirous of doing something to show their love for the young creature, who received their smallest attention with heartfelt gratitude. The Colonel was always thinking of something that would add to her comfort. It was either a new easy chair, a rare painting, or a choice engraving—always something new and diverting. Lloyd would drop in and while away an hour in pleasant chat. The Count brought her favorite authors, and read to her for hours, sometimes stealing a stealthy glance at the rose which deepened upon the white cheek for one short moment, and then faded. Laura and Nellie robbed the gardens and conservatories of their choicest treasures, which were laid as an offering of love before Claire, who repaid each with a sweet kiss. Jim and the cook did their part also. Never were choicer delicacies prepared to tempt the palate of an invalid than those which found their way to Claire's room. And Isabelle, who seldom visited the sick-room, now asked, in a cold, formal manner, each morning, after Claire's health. Drs. Singleton and Thorne called each day, more from force of habit than that Claire required their professional services.

Count Sayvord watched Dr. Singleton with interest. Reason as he would, he could not divest himself of the thought that the Doctor knew something of Claire's parents. Times without number he had determined to seek the old gentleman's confidence, and as many times gave it up, from the fear that his intentions might be misconstrued.

Dr. Singleton regarded young Sayvord with a friendly eye, and thought he should like to know more of him. "Who knows," thought the Doctor, "but he may have met Richard Tracy somewhere during his years of travel, or may know some one that has seen him! And I may be enabled to get trace of him; for at this rate, the confession of Manville is likely to lie in my private drawer for a century to come." An opportunity soon presented itself, which was improved by the Doctor.

During a pause in the conversation, he asked the Count if he had ever met an American gentleman by the name of Tracy during his lengthy travels.

"Years ago," replied the young man, "I met a gentleman of that name at my Uncle Sayvord's country-seat. Richard Tracy was the name; I remember well. He was a thoughtful, sad-browed man, over whose life a shadow seemed to have fallen."

"The same! the same!" exclaimed the Doctor, excitedly. "Have you heard any thing of him since—or do you know where he is now?"

"I received a letter from him about six weeks ago, and am expecting another by every mail. He is at present at my Uncle Clayburn Sayvord's, in the southern part of France."

"Can it be possible!" ejaculated the Doctor. "Will you allow me to see the letter you received from Richard?"

"Certainly," replied the Count, passing him the letter.

"The same clear, manly hand," said the Doctor, glancing at the superscription, as he proceeded to read the contents of the letter. When finished, he again turned to the young man, saying:

"So you too had a suspicion of the truth; for Claire Neville is indeed the daughter of Richard Tracy, and grand-daughter of the Colonel."

"Let there be full confidence between us, Doctor," said the Count. "Tell me of her mother; for there is a secret somewhere which I have failed to ferret out."

Dr. Singleton looked very thoughtful for a moment, and then replied, very gravely:

"Count Sayvord, if you will first answer truthfully two questions which I shall ask, I will cheerfully tell you all I know." The Count readily assured him that he would answer to the best of his ability any question he might ask.

The Doctor hesitated a moment, and then abruptly asked:

"Do you *love* Claire Neville? Do you wish to make her your wife? Or—"

"Enough, sir!" angrily interrupted Sayvord. "I did not expect this. Such questions are intrusive."

"I beg your pardon, if I have offended you," replied the Doctor, courteously, "but, believe me, I was actuated by no idle curiosity."

The Count, somewhat mollified, felt a little ashamed of his hasty temper. The truth was, he had never analyzed his feelings toward Claire. But the Doctor's question told him that he did love her with the whole depths of his ardent nature.

"I do love Claire—and if she will accept me, I will make her my wife, beloved and honored above woman."

The Doctor grasped the young man's hand and shook it warmly.

"That is the right kind of talk. None of your sentimental nonsense for me. I am a plain man, and always express my thoughts in the plainest phrases. I have foreseen all this for some time, and have thus seemingly interfered with your private business to prevent trouble hereafter, and, perhaps, a great deal of unhappiness to both parties. Caste has proved the bane of Richard Tracy's life. It may prove the bane of yours."

Sayvord was somewhat mystified by the Doctor's language.

The old man continued:

"Richard Tracy's wife, the mother of Claire Neville, was a *quadroon* and once a *slave*, owned by her own *father*, and sold by *him* to Colonel Tracy."

Sayvord was greatly excited at this revelation, and exclaimed:

"Impossible, Doctor! You are laboring under some mistake!"

"Not a bit of it!" was the emphatic reply, and he related the entire history of Richard's life. When concluded, he remarked, "I have told you these facts, that you may accustom yourself to thinking of them—and if you marry Claire Neville, you do so with a full knowledge of her origin; and, knowing these facts, if you give her up, you alone are the sufferer, and she is spared the bitter knowledge that caste is the bane of her life's happiness."

The Count had been swayed by various emotions during the Doctor's narrative. He now sat thoughtful and silent. He at last said slowly:

"I must think of this, Doctor. It is best to accustom one's self to look unpleasant facts steadily in the face, and I thank you for your forethought."

"And now," said Dr. Singleton, "let us talk of Richard Tracy. He is, or was, when last heard from, with your uncle, in France."

"Yes," replied the Count; "but if he is not already, he soon will be, on his way to America, for I have written him to come without delay."

"All the better. I hope he will come—"

The sentence remained unfinished, for at this moment Jim entered the room, and said, with an overwhelming bow:

"A letter for de Count Sayvord."

The Count hastily broke the seal, and read the almost unintelligible scrawl, exclaiming, as he roughly shook the Doctor's arm:

"My uncle and Richard Tracy are in New Orleans at this moment."

CHAPTER XXXI.   September 23, 1865

Strange Events.

The meeting between Dr. Singleton and Richard was an affecting one. The first greeting over, the doctor held Richard at arm's length, and surveyed him scrutinizingly. He could not realize that the beardless boy he had bade adieu eighteen years before had returned to him after these years, a prematurely old man. He could hardly realize that this bearded, sad-browed man, with form slightly bent, was the young Richard, over whose couch of suffering he had watched for days and weeks.

Richard read the doctor's thoughts, and asked, with a sad smile: "Am I, then, changed so much?"

"Time and sorrow has indeed dealt hardly with you, my boy," and the old man's voice was low and trembled with sadness.

Monsieur Sayvord presented the Count to Richard, and Monsieur, in turn, was presented to Dr. Singleton.

Claire's advent in the Tracy family, her late illness, Manville's death, Col. Tracy's pride and prejudices, were the subjects under discussion. All except Richard thought that the Colonel's pride was pretty well subdued. A sigh of relief escaped Richard as Dr. Singleton related the closing scenes of Manville's life.

"It is well," he repeated, softly. And the trio knew well of what he was thinking.

Richard was impatient to see his daughter, but it was thought best that in her present weak state, she should be somewhat prepared to meet her father.

"I will undertake that task," said the doctor. "Her life is too precious to be periled by a sudden and indiscreet disclosure!" and he glanced significantly at the Count, who flushed slightly. Richard's eyes followed that glance, and he read its possible meaning, while his tried heart uttered the prayer—

"God spare my child the ordeal through which I have passed!"

It was decided that the doctor should inform Claire of the arrival of her father. There was a more difficult task to be performed. Who was to convey the intelligence to the irascible father? The Count and Monsieur Sayvord undertook that mission, and felt hopeful of the result.

"I will write a few lines which I wish you to bear to my mother," said Richard, addressing the Count, who promised to deliver it to Mrs. Tracy.

"But that confession of Manville's, doctor, when will you bring it?"

"Early to-morrow morning, or, on his return, Monsieur Sayvord will bring it this evening."

The three gentlemen took their departure, leaving Richard to the company of his own thoughts, but first bidding him be of good cheer, and hope that all would yet be well.

Claire had awaked from her long, refreshing sleep, and was wondering what kept Mrs. Tracy from her side so long. Then she thought of Col. Tracy's manner towards her, so full of remorseful tenderness, and wondered if she was indeed his grandchild. And if she were, where could her father be? Was it not strange he never made inquiry concerning her? But perhaps he did not care to find her. And ere she knew it, Claire was weeping piteously.

In a little while she became composed, and for the first time since her illness, thought over the exciting scenes of that short interval preceding her loss of reason. She recalled her conversation with the dying Manville, and she murmured softly,

"My poor father was cruelly wronged, and my delicate young mother hastened to a premature grave. How he must have loved her and mourned her early death. No one ever loved me. It must be happiness to know that some one is always thinking of one's comfort. I do wish father would come. I think Col. Tracy would forgive him."

It was the hour the Count usually came in to read, but this afternoon he came not. Even little Nellie failed to make her accustomed visit. What did it mean? Had every one deserted her? Her quick ear caught the sound of wheels and the steps of several persons entering the hall. She heard steps ascending the stairs and pass to the library. Next she heard some one approaching her door, and the genial face of Dr. Singleton peered into the apartment. Seeing Claire awake, he entered. Taking a seat by her side, he took the white and almost transparent hand in his, saying,

"How do you feel this afternoon, dear?"

"I am feeling quite well, doctor, only a little weak, you know," replied Claire, with a cheerful smile.

"I am glad to hear it," replied the doctor, "Now tell me what you have been thinking of this long afternoon?"

"Oh, a great many things, doctor! I have been thinking of my father and my mother, and also of Manville's death, and how kind every one is to me. And I was wondering if Colonel Tracy would forgive my father if he should return."

"I trust he would," was the doctor's fervent reply.

"You knew my father very well, did you not?" asked Claire, eagerly.

"Yes, dear," was the quiet reply.

"Is it very long since you saw him?"

"Not long," returned the doctor, evasively, while a queer smile played upon his lips.

Claire was looking straight into the old gentleman's eyes, when she said,

"But tell me how long. Just exactly how long ago it was?"

"Why, how exacting you have grown, little one," he said, smiling. "But tell me, would you like to see your father very much?"

"Would I," repeated Claire, "how can you ask me?"

"Well, Claire, if you will promise me not to become excited, nor make yourself sick with asking questions, I will tell you a secret."

"I promise," replied Claire, eagerly, a thousand thoughts thronging her mind in an instant.

"Well, Claire, your father *has come*, and you shall see him soon."

Claire remembered her promise, and, with a desperate effort, controlled her feelings, and asked, quietly:

"When can I see him, doctor?"

"As early to-morrow morning as you wish."

She was forced to be satisfied, and asked:

"Who knows of his arrival besides yourself?"

"Count Sayvord, whose uncle arrived this morning with Richard."

"Did Count Sayvord know my father?" she asked.

"He saw your father some years ago at his uncle's, in France. But it is owing to the Count that he has returned to New Orleans. Your resemblance to Richard Tracy first attracted his attention, and he wrote to his uncle concerning you, and asking about Richard. Your father saw the letter. Others followed, and the result is that Richard Tracy is now in New Orleans, seeking his daughter."

Dr. Singleton soon took leave of his young friend, promising to call early, with her father, the following morning. Claire sank back upon the crimson cushions, her pale cheeks flushed with excitement. An hour passed, and no one came, until Rose brought in the tea-tray.

"Rose, where is Mrs. Tracy?"

"Don't know, Miss Claire, I'm sure. There's great times 'bout this house to-day. The missus fainted away in old Mattie's arms this afternoon. I was going through the hall, and heard a scream for help. I thought the sound came from the east room. I went in. There sat Mattie, on the floor, crying over missus, who looked as white and lifeless as a piece of linen. We worked hard with her a long time. She had just revived so as to be able to sit up and talk a little, when a knock was heard at the door. I opened it, and there stood Count—what's his name?"

"Sayvord," interposed Claire.

"Oh, never mind the name," said Rose. "He had a note for Mrs. Tracy. I handed it to her. When she looked at the writing, I thought she was going to faint again. But she didn't. Old Mattie asked: 'Missus, is it from him?' 'Yes,' she said, 'it is. I am going to him. Tell Jim to get the carriage ready. I wish to go out.' And away she went, and hasn't come back yet. That young Count and a funny little old man are up in the library with massa now. Mattie's crying, in the east room, fit to break her heart. Jim looks awful wise, and Dinah's as cross as fury. I don't see what the house is coming to," repeated Rose, as she passed out.

"And I am happy," murmured Claire.

Two Alternate Conclusions to *The Curse of Caste*

The Happy Ending

After her tearful but joyous reunion with her father, Claire learns from him that her mother was a noble, refined, and pure woman, as Claire had always hoped would be true. Although the story of her mother's death moves Claire deeply, she is inspired by the knowledge that Lina Tracy was a loyal and faithful wife. When her father tells her about her mother's enslavement and African American heritage, Claire is shocked to think that such an injustice could occur, but she is not horrified at the realization that she too is mixed race. The "darkly beautiful" Claire reveals to her father that even in girlhood, her color had given her intimations of a difference from other children, that Juno, her nurse, never tried to deny. Arriving at the Tracys' New Orleans estate and finding herself to be "an object of curiosity even to the negroes," Claire could not help but ponder her mysterious origins of "poverty and misfortune."

The knowledge that explains these questions, combined with her long-standing affection for Juno, allow Claire to accept the news of her racial heritage without self-pity or recrimination. Although she has expressed no direct disapproval of slavery before, the news that her mother was once a slave and that her father almost died rather than disavow her elicits from Claire words of moral indignation against slavery.

After father and daughter finish talking over the process that brought them together, they return to the Tracy family to share the joy of their reunion. With Claire as intermediary, Frank and Richard Tracy are reconciled. Only Isabelle seems unmoved by the embrace of father and son.

As the family prepare for a celebratory banquet, Count Sayvord asks Claire for leave to speak with her alone. In the quiet drawing room, he declares his love and asks Claire for her hand. Unprepared, Claire confesses her attraction to the Count but predicates her answer to his proposal on her informing him of her mixed racial background. He replies that he has already known about her family past and has decided it is irrelevant to his love or his plans for their wedded future. He knows that in America a "curse of caste" could threaten their love, but he wants to take Claire away from the United States to a new home, the Sayvord family estate in France. Claire accepts Sayvord's proposal.

At the family banquet the couple announce their intentions to marry and move to France. While Frank Tracy comforts the disappointed Isabelle, Richard congratulates the Count. Claire urges her father to return with the couple to France. He gladly accepts her offer. The story ends with the departure of Claire, Sayvord, and Richard Tracy for Europe, with the full blessing of the Tracy family in New Orleans.

Editors' Comment

Conclusion One represents the best-case scenario for a conventional happy ending to *The Curse of Caste*. Such an ending rewards Claire in traditional fashion for her traditional goodness, via marriage to a noble man who proves that he can and will eschew caste prejudice. The revelation that her innocent mother was once enslaved could allow Claire at the end of the story to espouse antislavery, at least verbally. Having created Claire with little evident social conscience, Collins could use her realization of her mother's enslavement to give Claire at least the opportunity to speak a word against slavery and caste, although it is unlikely that Claire in the last scene of the novel would match her father's outspoken repudiation of the Tracy family's involvement in slavery earlier in the story. While

Claire may declare herself shocked by the injustice of slavery against her mother, the happy ending that Collins could have chosen would still entail Claire's choosing what Collins termed woman's "sacred office," wifehood and motherhood, rather than a career in antislavery work.

It is possible, of course, that Collins could have planned for Claire to reject the Count's proposal, preferring instead to have her remain single and become, like Collins herself, a teacher. Such a career choice would mean, however, that Claire's ties to the various characters in the novel she most loves would be severely strained. Could a self-identified African American teacher continue to live with the slaveholding Tracy family? If not, where would she go? Whom would she teach? The novel offers no basis for Claire's taking such a radical step out of the only social world she has known in her adult life.

Marrying Claire to Sayvord would have allowed Collins to reconfirm the legitimacy of interracial marriage in the novel. By sending Claire and Sayvord back to Europe, however, this conclusion of the novel would not require them to challenge American racism head-on. Claire's decision to accept Sayvord's proposal follows the example of her father, who chose love over caste considerations. But by exporting the marriage to France, Collins allows Claire to follow her father, who resided happily at the Sayvord estate while in exile after his wounding, albeit in a less socially rebellious way. This would be consistent with Collins's conservative views of womanhood in general.

Thus Claire's marriage would not separate her from her long-lost father, to whom she has just been reunited in the final chapters of the novel. Instead, marriage to the Count allows Claire to become a wife and mother while attesting a proper daughterly duty to her father. This reinforces Claire's role in the novel as a nurturing domestic ideal who restores and reintegrates her father's family while anticipating potential motherhood of her own.

The Tragic Ending

After her tearful but joyous reunion with her father, Claire learns from him that her mother was a noble, refined, and pure woman, as Claire had always hoped would be true. Although the story of her mother's death moves Claire deeply, she is inspired by the knowledge that Lina Tracy was a loyal and faithful wife. When her father tells her about her mother's enslavement and African American heritage, Claire is shocked to think that such an injustice could occur, but she is not horrified at the realization that she too is mixed race. The "darkly beautiful" Claire reveals to her father that even in girlhood, her color had given her intimations of a difference from other children, that Juno, her nurse, never tried to deny. Arriving at the Tracys' New Orleans estate and finding herself to be "an object of curiosity even to the negroes," Claire could not help but ponder her mysterious origins of "poverty and misfortune."

The knowledge that explains these questions, combined with her long-standing affection for Juno, allow Claire to accept the news of her racial heritage without self-pity or recrimination. Although she has expressed no direct disapproval of slavery before, the news that her mother was once a slave and that her father almost died rather than disavow her elicits words of moral indignation against slavery from Claire.

After father and daughter finish talking over the process that brought them together, they prepare to return to the rest of the family to share the joy of their reunion. But on the way to the dining room, Count Sayvord asks Claire for leave to speak with her alone. In the quiet drawing room, he declares his love and asks Claire for her hand. Unprepared, Claire confesses her attraction to the Count but predicates her answer to his proposal on her informing him of her mixed racial background. He replies that he has already known about her family past and has decided it is irrelevant to his love or his plans for their wedded future. He knows that in America a "curse of caste" could threaten their love, but he wants to take Claire away from the United States to a new home, the Sayvord family estate in France.

At the moment that a smiling Claire seems on the verge of accepting the Count's proposal, Isabelle Tracy rushes into the room in a jealous rage. Having overheard the Count profess his love to Claire, Isabelle angrily accuses him of betraying her. Turning to Claire, the cold and cruel white woman denounces the governess as racially impure and morally corrupt, a threat to the future of the Tracy family and to the sanctity of Southern marriage. Drawing a pistol from a concealed pocket, Isabelle shoots the defenseless Claire.

Mortally wounded, Claire has but a few moments to speak. Surrounded by the distraught Tracy family, in her dying words Claire assures the count of her love, thanks the Tracys for their kindness and affection, and, most important, issues heartfelt forgiveness to Isabelle, who is moved to tearful, genuine remorse. Holding both her father's and her grandfather's hands, Claire expires, urging them to be fully and permanently reconciled for her sake as well as for that of the entire family. Each man promises to uphold the dying Claire's wishes.

Claire is buried on the Tracy estate. A brokenhearted Richard accepts his father's plea to remain in New Orleans but implores his father to free his slaves, arguing that it was "the fatal Nemesis of the South" that was ultimately responsible for Claire's as well as Lina's tragic deaths. A repentant Colonel Tracy agrees to emancipate his slaves.

Editors' Comment

Although Conclusion Two represents the worst-case scenario for *The Curse of Caste*, a number of references in the novel may have been intended as foreshadowings of a violent and tragic ending. The most prescient character in the novel, Juno, entreats Claire not to take the governess job in New Orleans: "Dear child, I fear you will see great sorrow." Later in the novel, the "glittering black eyes" of the jealous Isabelle "dilate with rage" toward Claire, expressing "volumes of hate" toward the increasingly fearful governess. By chapter XXIV Claire is so terrified by the sight of Isabelle that she shrieks, "'Those eyes are burning through my brain. Save me, oh, save me! She will kill me!'"

Such a violent death for Claire at the hands of her aunt Isabelle would recapitulate the near-violent death of Richard Tracy at the hands of his father, the Colonel. By having Claire actually die, however, Collins could transform her into an ultimately sacrificial figure, whose selfless, Christ-like death could heal the deepest self-inflicted wounds of the South, as symbolized by the internecine violence of the Tracy family.

Having Claire die at the hands of Isabelle would allow Collins to have her cake and eat it too, from a political standpoint. Sayvord's proposal and Claire's readiness to accept it would signal Collins's approval of the marriage of her second generation of interracial lovers. But by removing Claire before she could actually *be* married, Collins could finesse the problem that every other contemporary novelist who wrote about race mixing had to address: where could a mixed marriage take place, and, even more important in Claire's case, what sort of life should this seminary-trained, mixed-race heroine lead after marrying a French nobleman?

In the fall of 1865, a new day of freedom was dawning in her country as Collins brought her novel to its close. As she foresaw the conclusion of her novel the author must have struggled with uncertainties about whether Claire's marriage to Sayvord, however much that union might have appealed to her romantic side, would be acceptable to her *Christian Recorder* readers. If Collins believed, as she wrote in late December 1864, that national events were "changing the seemingly invincible destiny of our people, and building us up a nation," could she have been satisfied to limit her heroine's "sacred office" to wifehood and motherhood with a European nobleman?

Yet the logic of Collins's novel offers Claire little alternative to this marriage with Sayvord. Collins endows Claire with hardly any motive in the story other than doing good while hoping vaguely that she may somehow find out who her parents were. Collins's traditional evangelical values seem clearly at work in her portrayal of Claire as the redemptive angel-in-the-house, an ideal nineteenth-century Victorian lady, which Collins's *Christian Recorder* readers would have favored even as they savored Claire's unintentional (and therefore more delicious) defeat of her proud white female rival in love. But given Claire's slight degree of socio-political consciousness or special concern for African Americans (enslaved or free), it is difficult to imagine how Collins could have suddenly redirected Claire's sense of purpose at the end of the novel away from matrimony.

Since Collins had not prepared her heroine for the future that the author could see African Americans facing in the fall of 1865, Collins may have felt she had no other choice but to have Claire die a redemptive death. Such an ending would have given Collins a way out of the dilemmas her story created for her, while underscoring once again the pathetic sacrifice and cruel human waste of America's "curse of caste." Collins could also salvage a political message from Claire's death by having her father, whose antislavery views are much more pronounced than Claire's (it is difficult to tell whether Claire is opposed to slavery at all), interpret her murder as yet another visitation of slavery's "nemesis" on the South and then press for the emancipation of his own father's slaves. Given the softening of the Colonel's attitudes toward race under Claire's quiet ministrations, not to mention his change of heart toward his son, the idea of Frank Tracy the emancipator would not be at all inconceivable as the final ending of *The Curse of Caste*.

THE ESSAYS OF JULIA C. COLLINS, 1864–65

MENTAL IMPROVEMENT.

It is a faulty and indolent humility that makes some of our people sit still and learn *nothing*, because they cannot learn everything. We are born with faculties and power, capable of almost anything. Who can measure our capacity, or set bounds to our progression in knowledge? Destitute alike of knowledge, the children of the white race have, in this respect, no advantage over the black; both have everything to learn. All must begin with the simplest elements of knowledge, and advance from step to step, in nearly the same manner. Much time and skill are requisite to mould the mind in strength and beauty, by proper exercise of its faculties. The mind is formed, gradually expanded and strengthened into vigorous action. We must subject ourselves to severe, and sometimes painful discipline, for this very exercise will enrich and embellish the mind with new and important ideas. We must feel that there is nothing too hard for industry and perseverance to accomplish. We must scale the rugged hill of science, by dint of powerful effort and great self-reliance, and at last reward ourselves by drinking at the richest streams of science and literature.

Happiness, as Pope remarks, is truly "Our being's end and aim!"[1] A mind well stored and well cultivated, is certainly conducive in every way to true happiness. What knowledge, ornamental and useful, we gain from a continued course of reading! We are made acquainted with passing events and occurrences in various parts of the world, and enabled to repeat the sentiments of those who existed in ages past, and offer to our reflection all the most important circumstances connected with the improvement of human society.

Among all persons distinguished for refinement and cultivation of the mind, the art of reading is the most prevalent and important. Not only the improvement of the mind, but the cultivation and purity of taste and the acquisition of knowledge, are the advantages derived from this art; and, while we read, we must think. We must combine anew the items of knowledge. We must reflect upon them often, and draw from them fresh influences and new truths for ourselves. It is only by such processes that we become truly intelligent.

Some persons of mature age have yet to learn to think well or reason clearly. Never imitate. It is better to acquire a clear practical way of thinking for ourselves, than to load the mind with a dead weight of other men's brains.

Let us each be a "unique," doing cheerfully, and faithfully that which is required of us, or for which we have a particular talent; and we cannot hope too much, or dare too much.

Williamsport, April 10th.

"Mental Improvement,"
Christian Recorder, vol. 4 (16),
April 16, 1864. New Series.
Whole No. 172:61.

SCHOOL TEACHING.

To teach successfully, two qualifications are indispensable, *i.e.,* tact and patience. Teachers should blend the character of instructor with that of a friend. The affection of your pupil once gained, you have their interest in every scheme for their improvement and advantage. Never give a child the impression or idea that you wish to rule over it, else from that moment there is tough warfare between you and that scholar. Be kind and gentle in your rule, but always firm, and even severe when the faithful discharge of your duty requires it. Speak kindly to your pupil; it will cost you nothing at most to deny yourself the satisfaction of reprimanding some little delinquent. A kind word of encouragement will often revive the drooping energies of some weary little one, and incite them to greater effort, to be crowned at last with success. Very few parents understand or appreciate the trials of the instructors of their children. They persist in saying, and perhaps in thinking a teacher has nothing to do but sit still and hear lessons. Oh! that is easy work, they say, and almost grudgingly pay their pittance required for the education of their children. I often wonder what mothers think when they allow a child to grow to the age of six or seven years without learning its letters, because they have not time, or it is too much trouble, or one out of a dozen other excuses, yet it is nothing for a teacher to perform their neglected duty. Asking and answering questions, hearing lessons, sometimes very indifferently recited, now solving some knotty problem for some puzzled little brain, now bending refractory fingers to the proper position in holding the pen, then those countless difficulties to be amicably adjusted, which occur at recess and other out of school hours. These and other duties too numerous to mention, comprise the daily and unchanging routine of a teacher's life. Yet they have nothing to do. But we teachers have our "lights" as well as our "shadows." And school-teaching is withal a pleasant business. A rent nicely mended in the frock of some incorrigible little romp will save a mother's time and patience, and the frightened delinquent a sharp scolding, and perhaps severe punishment. It costs you nothing but your time, and then you have won that child's gratitude, and gratitude is the antecedent of love to be demonstrated in a bunch of flowers, a rosy-cheeked apple, a piece of maple sugar, or whatever a child's fancy may suggest;—homely offerings, it is true. But how refreshing and encouraging to the weary heart of a teacher to feel that you have the love and respect of your pupils! The respectful "good morning and good afternoon, teacher," is pleasant to hear, and with it come a feeling of relief,—a night of rest to prepare for the duties of another day. Such, at least, is my experience as a teacher.

Williamsport, April 25th, 1864.

"School Teaching,"
Christian Recorder, vol. 4 (19),
May 7, 1864. New Series.
Whole No. 175:73.

INTELLIGENT WOMEN.

In this, the dawn of the colored man's "golden era," when the dark cloud, which for ages has enveloped in darkness the destiny of our race, is rapidly revealing its "silver lining" to many an anxious and expectant heart; and the time is coming, with giant strides, when the black man will have only to assert his equality with the white, to have it fully and cordially awarded to him.

The spirit of improvement, and self-elevation, which is animating the greater mass of our people, is truly encouraging and commendable. But it is not of this, I would speak! Few, thoughtful or observant persons, can fail to have noted the great number of good-looking, and *naturally* intelligent young girls, who never spend a thought but upon dress and pleasure. Who never spend one hour in trying to improve or cultivate their minds, while hour after hour, of precious time, is frittered away in idleness and gayety. If these thoughtless young creatures would only consider that every hour wasted, is a brilliant lost, which dims the lustre of life's jewel-time,—I am sure their course would be far different. And our Creator never endowed us with sound minds, strong and vigorous faculties, that we should let them rest, passive and inert, for want of proper energy and ambition, if not a better motive; but that we should improve and increase the talents He has given us, that we may become good and useful members of society; that we may become able to benefit our fellow-creatures, and through them, be benefited again. We should improve every opportunity that is offered for our moral and intellectual culture; not only for the pure enjoyment, and gratification it affords; not merely as a matter of taste; but it is incumbent upon us, as a duty.

It is woman's province to make home happy, to be man's companion, at once tried and true; to be the mother, and instructor of his children; and this is what every woman should prepare herself to become, and render herself worthy to fulfill the sacred office of wife and mother. A refined and intelligent woman is certainly more companionable than a coarse and uncultivated one. Girls, remember that intelligent and well-informed young men, seek the company of intelligent young ladies. And the young man that would make just the husband you would be proud to own, would very likely choose a wife possessing some qualities of which he, too, may be proud.

It is a noticeable fact, that which too many young ladies value so lightly, as a self-attribute, they are quick to detect, and appreciate, in the opposite sex, and a young man of refined and cultivated manners, is always best received. *Vice versa*, the uncouth and ignorant, are looked upon with most consummate scorn by these self-constituted judges of merit. And I would ask, "Why is this the case?"

It would seem as though that which we admire, and think beautiful in another, we would seek to win for ourselves.

Now, my dear young friends, listen to the advice of one who is closely allied with you by caste and misfortune. Improve your time, and you will never have cause to regret your choice.

O rouse thee, then . . .
Extend, improve, enjoy the hours of life,
Assert thy reason, animate thy heart,
And act, through life's short scene, the useful part.
TALBOT.[1]

Williamsport, May 29th.

"Intelligent Women,"
Christian Recorder, vol. 4 (23),
June 4, 1864. New Series.
Whole No. 179:89.

A LETTER FROM OSWEGO[1]:
ORIGINALITY OF IDEAS.

Most persons who desire to talk well, read a great deal from ancient and modern writers, with the view of becoming brilliant conversationalists. But it too frequently happens they read much and think little, and when conversing with them, you are favored with quotations from this author and that, till the sayings of our good old writers become, as it were, hackneyed phrases. Not that I would seek to annul the great benefits derived from a proper course of reading, or the storing of the mind with useful facts and brilliant gems of thought, taken, as it were, from the mental ore of some gifted mind.

It is good to read, but better to think. It is well to select our reading matter from the best authors, and while absorbed with interest in the workings of a master-mind, close the book and carefully review with the mind's eye, that which we have just read. While thus communing with our thoughts, we involuntarily and unconsciously contrast and compare our ideas with the author's, and from the chaos of the mind comes forth new and beautiful thoughts, "original ideas," gems not another's finding, but as the reward of this effort of self-culture. I would say to the student and reader, acquire all the knowledge, useful and ornamental, that you can, and it matters not from what source, only let your own mind be properly exercised upon all subjects, and not weighed down with a dead mass of other men's brains, until from habitual inaction, the mind becomes inert and utterly prostrated, quite incapable of clear thought or sound reasoning. But this evil has a specific remedy, for that which habitual to us we soon learn to love. If we have one hour to spend, it is best to spend only half that time in reading, and the remaining half hour in carefully reviewing what we have read, dissect the thoughts and sentiments of the authors, trying to catch something of the writer's spirit. Let your mind run parallel with his, and you will elucidate charms before unnoticed, you will find it entertaining and interesting, as well as instructive.

If we pursue this course, our knowledge acquired from various sources is well diversified with ideas of our own, and our conversation will seldom lack interest; we should be able to form our own ideas and opinions upon all subjects worthy of thought. But here the opposite error presents itself, and should be as sedulously guarded against as should originality be cultivated. Too much singularity of opinion savors of eccentricity, and that is not a desirable attribute. We should offer our ideas, when called for, with modest diffidence. Originality is possessed by few; and why? Because we neglect self-culture, because we are too ready, too willing to depend upon the brain-work of others, till we lose our mental identity, till our originality of thought is lost in the chaos of odds and ends of other men's sentiments. We certainly have "brain" or talent, why not use it? It may lie buried beneath the accumulated dust of years of inaction, no matter, better late than not all; hunt up every lost idea and every stray thought. You will find them in odd nooks and corners of the brain: it only requires careful research to bring them forth. Now let us try and bring about a reformation of habits and tastes; let us dig deep and study hard, and our reward will be "originality."

Oswego, N.Y., Dec. 2nd, 1864.

"A Letter From Oswego:
Originality of Ideas,"
Christian Recorder, vol. 4 (50),
December 10, 1864. New Series.
Whole No. 206:198.

"LIFE IS EARNEST."[1]

"Life is real!" And, now that the New Year dawns for us so beautifully, let us begin life anew, and learn to live in earnest! The old year
has been fraught with real and important changes and events—
events that have far towered—changing the seemingly invincible
destiny of our people, and building us up a nation that shall shine
forth as a star on the breast of time, and be gathered into the brilliant galaxy of great nations! There is a vast work for us to do! We
have not a moment to lose! We have gone through life dreaming
too long! We must become aroused, shake off the dead lethargy of
inaction, and go to work in earnest! And there is no time so fitting
to begin as with the new year. We have all a mission here on earth,
which is, to do all the good we can! It is a solemn thing to fritter
away life aimlessly—to be content with mere existence—to have
no higher aspirations, no greater hope of good hereafter! We may
be surrounded with the necessaries and even the luxuries of life;
kind friends may surround us; we may enjoy life; but, there comes
to us all an inward longing, longing; a kind of remorseful dissatisfaction with ourselves: there is a void, and we feel it, and are vainly
seeking and craving after some thing that is intangible. It is the
craving for a better, the yearning of the soul after a truer, higher,
and nobler existence! We want food for the soul, and healthy un-
tiring employment for the mind! We will be no longer dreamers,
but workers, in the field of life! We will build no more air castles,
to see them crumble in ruins at our feet or vanish as the morning
mists that mantle the gliding stream! Oh, no! we will live in earnest; we will be true to ourselves, our better natures and our God.
Another year is gone—has rolled into the irreclaimable and irre-
trievable past; and yet we live, endowed with health and strength,
while many who stood with us, filled with hope and happiness,
on the last new year, have entered that "bourn from whence no
traveler returns,"[2] and we are spared! For what? Not, certainly, to

be drifted through life by every passing current until we reach the gulf-stream and are swallowed up in the yawning depths of eternity. No! We have been spared another year, perhaps, to improve the time and talent God has given us, working out his divine will; for it is the will of God that we become a nation and a people; and He is bringing us out of the "depths" to the dazzling heights of liberty, where the very air is resonant with freedom. God's ways are inscrutable and mysterious! But let us wait with patience for the end, let us work faithfully, leaving the result with Him who rules the destinies of nations, and "all will be well!" We must not anticipate the future too much, but be satisfied that the future will bring a suitable reward. Too much anticipation of the "good time coming"[3] disinclines us for present action. *Our* future, now, will soon be our present, which will soon resolve itself into the past, and we still have the future before us dark and impenetrable as ever! We have naught to do with but the present! We will take care of the minutes, the golden sands of life, which we lose so easily, and hours, days and weeks, will take care of themselves, while months are woven together till another year—another golden link is formed in the circuit of man's allotted time. As this may be the last new year, let us hasten to reform, and, hereafter, feel that life is earnest, and it is incumbent upon us that we live for some noble purpose, some object worthy of our efforts.

Oswego, Dec. 23d, 1864.

"Life Is Earnest,"
Christian Recorder, vol. 5 (1),
January 7, 1865. New Series.
Whole No. 209:1.

MEMORY AND IMAGINATION.

These twin beauties of the mind render the brain a miniature world. What beautiful pictures memory sketches from the pages of the past, while imagination solves and renders them replete with living beauty. Beautiful memory, how lightly we value this grand and sublime attribute of the mind. By the aid of memory we are enabled to review the past, from our infancy. We may dwell long and lovingly over the sweet scenes of our childhood, as fond recollection presents them to view. We may stand again on the threshold of the world, when we gazed on the trials of life through a golden cloud, when we were eager to take up the responsibilities of men and women, to mingle with the gay world. But a change has come o'er the spirit of our dreams.[1] Would that we could now look on life as in our childlike days of innocence. We have realized that life is more than a passing dream. A stern reality, even in our dreams saddened memory brings the light of other days around us, and visions of happiness dance over the mind, wearied forms press in quaint review down the shadowy vistas of the past. In sweet dreamlight memory reproduces the lights and loves of the far away time, and imagination beautifies and lends a fairylike enchantment to the scene; but memory deals not always thus gently with us, for she sometimes persists in unlocking the ghost-haunted chambers of the brain, and bringing out the skeleton we have hidden, and fain would forget. And out of these chambers come troops of spirits with dark, foreboding aspects, to act over again some dark scene in life's drama, some act the recollection of which we are vainly seeking to bury in oblivion; but they are engraved on the tablet of memory, and, while reason remains shall haunt our visions and the skeleton remains in the far away corner of the brain to be reproduced perhaps in our brightest hours, or happiest moments. Here, too, imagination, faithful ever to memory, points to a future so dark and foreboding that we shudder for a moment of calm forgetfulness, neither is memory always thus avenging, for she smoothes with gentle and soothing influence the sad recollections of parting scenes with the dearly loved, who have long since passed away from earth, away to happier homes, where parting and sorrow are no more. Gentle imagination tones down the high coloring till all is sweet harmony, and the heart of man is chastened and subdued by the memory of such sorrows long since passed away, but ever to remain fresh in the casket of remembrances. It is well we cannot forget it. The recollection ever restrains the wayward and erring, while imagination is an important auxiliary that presents these brain pictures in such vivid and striking colors, such a contrast of light and shadow as become indelibly stamped on the heart, and we would have these pictures always beautiful, such as we would love to look upon and linger over, after they have been retouched by the hand of time. We must regulate our actions so that in the time to come there may be no dark foreboding scenes to be drawn by memory, that imagination, ever busy, may not even in our dreams, haunt us with accusing visions. If we steadfastly practise the "Golden Rule,"[2] let it guide and govern our lives; we shall have few dark pictures to mourn over, while sweet memory and beautiful imagination shall vie with each other in gilding our path through life with sunshine and happiness. Then let us love and follow the golden precept, which says: "Do unto others as you would that others should do unto you."

Owego,[3] January 20th, 1865.

"Memory and Imagination,"
Christian Recorder, vol. 5 (4),
January 28, 1865. New Series.
Whole No. 212:14.

Questions for Discussion

1. What is it that motivates Claire Neville most strongly from the beginning of *The Curse of Caste*? Although a young woman with a pleasing personality, a striking appearance, and an unusual amount of education, she still feels herself lacking in something key to making a satisfying start in life. What is it?

2. What makes Claire appeal so strongly to the Tracy family after she has begun to work for them as a governess? Why do even the slaves care so much about her welfare?

3. Why is Isabelle Tracy so resentful of Claire? In light of all Isabelle's advantages, why should she become so malicious toward the governess?

4. Colonel Frank Tracy seems to be Julia Collins's personification of the Southern slave-holding aristocrat in *The Curse of Caste*. Besides his staunch defense of slavery itself, what other qualities does the author endow him with in order to characterize the slave-holding point of view?

5. What is the significance of the Colonel's growing conviction in the novel that Claire is his granddaughter? What effect does this conviction have on his character? Why would Julia Collins allow her archdefender of slavery to develop in this way?

6. What qualities does Richard Tracy have in common with his father? How do they differ, beyond the fact that they are diametric opposites on the slavery issue? How does the plot of *The Curse of Caste* bring father and son back together? Do you think they would have reconciled in the end, had Collins lived to finish the story?

7. Lina Hartly has no idea that she is a slave when she meets her future husband on the Mississippi riverboat that conveys them both to New Orleans early in the story. Why has that knowledge been kept from her? Why would Colonel Tracy refer to her in chapter VI as a member of "this sensitive class of negroes"?

8. In some ways Juno Hays is the most original character in the novel. Unassuming but very insightful, Juno, the author hints, was once enslaved but gained her freedom and created a fulfilling life for herself in Connecticut. What qualities of Juno ensure that she will play such a positive role in the story? What kind of statement was Julia Collins attempting to make about African American women through the characterization of Juno Hays?

9. Why does Lina Tracy not survive in the novel, while Juno Hays does?

10. What do you think Count Sayvord means when he tells Dr. Singleton in chapter XXIX that "It is best to accustom one's self to look unpleasant facts steadily in the face." What "unpleasant facts" is he talking about?

11. Do you think Collins intended to have Count Sayvord propose marriage to Claire Neville at the end of the novel? Why or why not?

12. Which of the two likely endings to *The Curse of Caste* proposed by the editors seems most fitting to you? Do you think Collins, as an African American woman author in 1865, would have chosen the ending that you feel is most fitting?

13. Why was the freedom for African American women to marry in defiance of "the curse of caste" so important to Julia Collins? Given the many social injustices brought about by slavery and caste consciousness in America in 1865, why do you think the first African American woman novelist chose to focus on the rights of African American women to marry whomever they loved, even if he was white?

14. Does *The Curse of Caste* idealize interracial love, or does the novel portray it realistically? What effect, if any, does Collins's situation in 1865 have on your judgment of the novel?

15. How is *The Curse of Caste* similar to, or different from, other novels by black and white American women from the mid- to late nineteenth century? Does Collins address comparable themes, or use similar voice and plot devices as Frances E. W. Harper, Harriet Beecher Stowe, or other more or less contemporary authors?

16. Since so little is known about Julia Collins's life, what would you like to know about her that you think might help you to understand what she was trying to accomplish with her novel?

17. Does *The Curse of Caste* remind you of any modern stories you have read? What are the similarities and differences?

18. Do you see any clues in Julia Collins's essays that might help us to speculate about the details of her life, her identity, and her writing of *The Curse of Caste*?

Chapter I

1. A place of learning or training in the nineteenth century, such as a preparatory school or college.
2. In Roman mythology, the goddess of women and protector of marriage.

Chapter II

1. Someone who suffers from hypochondria, a state of anxiety or depression about one's own health. Hoyden: a tomboy.

Chapter IV

1. A common phrase of invocation or calling to a number of people, such as in "A New Year's Address" (from *Robert Merry's Museum*, January 1846, 1–3): "Come, Girls and Boys—Black Eyes and Blue— / And hear a story made for you."
2. Bearing, especially as registered in facial expression.

Chapter V

1. This popular aphorism stems from a Latin proverb that appeared in English as early as the late fourteenth century in William Langland's *The Vision of Piers Plowman* B 11, 37–38.
2. A Moorish palace in Grenada, Spain, constructed in the fourteenth century.

Chapter VI

1. The Greek god of the underworld. Also the classical Greek name for the underworld itself.
2. A woman of one-quarter African American racial heritage.
3. A disreputable woman, a prostitute at worst, a pert and uppity woman at best.

Chapter VII

1. Too much; unwanted.
2. A conifer that grows in New England, the Upper Midwest, Canada, and Alaska.

Chapter VIII

1. "The grass withereth, the flower fadeth; but the word of our God abideth for ever" (Isaiah 40:8).
2. Title of a popular poem, "Nature's Nobleman," by British didactic poet Martin Farquhar Tupper (1810–89): "Nature's own Nobleman, friendly and frank, / Is a man with his heart in his hand!"
3. Proverbs 13:12.

Chapter IX

1. Regularly at intervals.
2. In Shakespeare's *Hamlet*, act 1, scene 5, Hamlet speaks these words in reference to his uncle, Claudius.

Chapter X

1. Hot-tempered; quick to anger.
2. Croesus, king of Lydia (560–546 BCE), was famed for his fabulous wealth.
3. In Greek myth, a goddess who dispenses divine justice and vengeance on humanity.

Chapter XI

1. A river flowing from Switzerland through Germany to the North Sea.

Chapter XIV

1. Ormolu, imitation gold leaf.
2. In the nineteenth century, Connecticut was known as "the land of steady habits" because of the reputedly strict morals of its inhabitants. New England was also characterized by this phrase in the nineteenth century.

Chapter XVI

1. The sun. In Greek mythology, Phoebus was an epithet of Apollo.

Chapter XVIII

1. In Greek mythology, Aesculapius, son of Apollo, was a physician.
2. A vain and conceited man.
3. A dissipated or debauched man.
4. Possibly the "indifferent mulatto girl" mentioned earlier in this chapter.

Chapter XIX

1. Alfred Lord Tennyson (1809–92), British poet laureate.

Chapter XX

1. A bedspread.

Chapter XXI

1. References to dancing. The quadrille is a French square dance performed by four couples. The quick-step refers to any quick dance.

Chapter XXII

1. A manservant.
2. Henry Brougham (1778–1868), British politician who led the effort to pass the 1833 antislavery act that abolished slavery throughout the British colonies.

Chapter XXIII

1. Apothecary, a nineteenth-century druggist.
2. In dancing, a whirl or spin on one foot.
3. Dancing. See John Milton's classic lyric poem "L'Allegro" (1645): "Come, and trip it, as you go / On the light fantastic toe."

Chapter XXIV

1. Inflammation of the brain.

Chapter XXV

1. A structure often built over a stream to serve as a dairy or larder.
2. To go quickly.

Chapter XXVI

1. A port city in the Normandy region of northern France.
2. A popular expression meaning to tour the local points of interest in a particular place.
3. A small city in Connecticut about thirty miles northeast of New York City.

Chapter XXVIII

1. Customary or usual.
2. Young hens.

"Mental Improvement"

1. Alexander Pope (1688–1744), English poet, critic, and satirist. See Pope's *Essay on Man* (1733–34), epistle 4, line 1.

"Intelligent Women"

1. From "Poetry," lines 59–62 by British poet Catharine Talbot (1721–70).

"A Letter From Oswego"

1. A town in upstate New York on the southern shore of Lake Ontario.

"Life Is Ernest"

1. Life is Real! Life is Earnest!" begins the second stanza of "A Psalm of Life" (1838) by the popular American poet Henry Wadsworth Longfellow (1807–82).
2. William Shakespeare, *Hamlet*, act 1, scene 5, 104.
3. A possible allusion to the novel *The Good Time Coming* (1855) by popular American writer Timothy Shay Arthur (1809–85) or to "There's a Good Time Coming," a song made popular by the Hutchinson Family, which crusaded against slavery and espoused various reforms through its singing performances in the United States and England during the mid-nineteenth century. See John W. Hutchinson, *Story of the Hutchinsons* (1896).

"Memory and Imagination"

1. George Gordon, Lord Byron (1788–1824), British poet, "The Dream," stanza 3, line 75.
2. Do unto others as you would have them do unto you" (Matthew 7:12) is traditionally considered the Christian "Golden Rule."
3. A town in southern New York on the Susquehanna River.

ACKNOWLEDGMENTS

The editors thank the following friends and colleagues for their scholarly advice and sound criticism throughout the process of the making of this edition: Dickson D. Bruce, Gabrielle Foreman, Frances Smith Foster, Ruth Hodge, Joycelyn K. Moody, Colleen O'Brien, Carla L. Peterson, Eric Ledell Smith, Johnny Smith, and Veta Smith Tucker. Kari Winter was especially helpful with ideas about the conclusions of the novel. The editors extend special gratitude to Anne Bruder for her careful attention to the accurate renditions of Julia Collins's texts.

Mitch Kachun thanks Moira Ferguson and Sharon Harris for their enthusiastic reaction to *The Curse of Caste* and their early encouragement to pursue its publication. A National Endowment for the Humanities Summer Stipend in 2003 made possible the first foray into archival resources in Lycoming County, Pennsylvania, the Pennsylvania State Archives in Harrisburg, and other sites. In Williamsport, Pennsylvania, thanks to local historians Mamie Sweeting Diggs and Lou Hunsinger Jr.; Michael Figels and Paul Novak at Wildwood Cemetery; and the helpful staff and volunteers at the James V. Brown Library, the Thomas E. Taber Museum, and the Lycoming County Genealogical Society. I am especially grateful for the warm welcome and support of Constance Evadne Robinson, Rev. and Mrs. Kenneth Burnett, and the congregants of Williamsport's Bethel AME Church. As always, I must express my gratitude to Michelle Kachman and Silas Kachman for putting up with my academic obsessions, and to Karen Libman for sustaining me in all things.